Because of Mother's Prayer

by

Don Swinford

AuthorHouse™
1663 Liberty Drive, Suite 200
Bloomington, IN 47403
www.authorhouse.com
Phone: 1-800-839-8640

First published by AuthorHouse 6/21/2007

ISBN: 978-1-4343-1390-4 (sc)
ISBN: 978-1-4343-1575-5 (hc)

Printed in the United States of America
Bloomington, Indiana

This book is printed on acid-free paper.

Dedication

In my first book I specifically mentioned my wife, Marilyn, and my mother, Ruby, who contributed the most to my life. I would like to add to that list my father, Adren, who could find joy in many things when times were tough. His love of music and family and his dedication to that family was an example for all. He gave me a bright outlook on life for which I will always be thankful.

I'd also like to acknowledge the three persons who encouraged and assisted me in getting this novel ready for publication. It could not have happened without the help of my wife, the encouragement of a friend, Susan Murphy, and the editing assistance of Keven Peck.

Preface

In my first novel, "If We Never Meet Again This Side Of Heaven," a struggling mother loved, lost, and then found some of her children. She had loved them all with a mother's heart and for years was torn by being separated from them. It was the story of Frances. She was under-educated, married too young, and gave birth to seven children, only one of whom she would raise to maturity. Her children were Orville, nicknamed Orvie, Leo, William, Arthur, Theodore, Ursie, and Lloyd Edward. The family faced tragic trials and circumstances, but Frances' faith in God helped her keep her sanity and her desire to reunite her family. It was also the story of loving adoptive parents and how they came to adopt four of Frances' children.

Although the original story was fictional, loosely based on relatives of mine, people continually ask for a sequel giving more details of the boys growing up and what happened to them. My initial response was, "There is no sequel." This was the fictional story of a mother and what could have happened. After a few months, story lines started coming to me again and I found myself wanting to answer some of the questions about these lives that have existed only in my own mind. Did these brothers, some separated for over thirty years, truly bond? I gave up the fight and here is the sequel I vowed not to write.

Many of us are what we are today because of a mother's prayer. This continually guided my thoughts as I made up the lives, struggles, and victories recorded in this novel. I hope I have made it believable, as prayers do change lives. My own life is an example of that. How about you?

Contents

Chapter 1

꙾ ꙼

Reflections

From the first heartbeat of the child, until the last breath of the mother, her thoughts and prayers will be for her children. From the beginning of time, this has been true!

Never was this truer than in the life of Frances McGrew, the daughter of a Presbyterian minister born in near poverty in rural Illinois at the beginning of the twentieth century. As a child, she felt insignificant and unloved by her father, and therefore sought that love elsewhere at an early age. Her marriage brought her great happiness initially but it wasn't destined to last, as her first-born son was tragically taken from her early on. This loss was the beginning of the end of her marriage to Orville Trapp, although it struggled on for several years resulting in six more children.

Prayer was a constant in Frances' life after she married Orville. Her children became her life and when circumstances tore her family apart, prayer was all she had. She never lost her faith in God. Despite losing all of her children but one, four through adoption, she never lost hope of seeing her family reunited again. Through the most difficult depression years of the thirties and the devastating war years she grasped for any and all information of her lost children. This was to continue until her death in 1960.

Frances had lost two of her children, Orvie and Ursie when they were yet still toddlers, and after the war she learned of the loss of another, Arthur, killed in action in the war. She knew the reunion this side of Heaven was not going to happen, but she still had hopes for the remaining four. Through circumstances that can only be termed miraculous, she did find her three missing sons that had been adopted out in 1930 and got to know two of them before her death. Three of her sons were at her side when she died. She died too young and too soon without the total reunion she had prayed for so long, but William, Theodore, and Eddie were with her. One son, Leo was not.

William, her third son who had located her after the war, took it upon himself to make one last effort to reunite his brothers after his mother's death. William was the minister she had always prayed he would be. He had served as a chaplain during the war. It was William whose life was saved on a battlefield in Italy by a young medic. He didn't find out until later that the medic was his younger brother Arthur that he had been separated from in 1930. He did not find out about his brother soon enough, as Art died a hero's death caring for others on another battlefield before William could trace him down. Because of Art, William went back to rural Illinois to find Art's adoptive parents and tell them the story of their hero son and also to tell Art's birth mother about him. At this time he was reunited with his mother and met his future wife Molly, who had been Art's fiancée. Eventually this would result in his being reconnected with two other brothers, Ted and Eddie. Only upon Frances' death did he discover the information in the family Bible that led him to Leo, the missing brother.

Leo was the son that didn't want to be found. He was the oldest of the surviving Trapp boys and had grown up feeling betrayed by the family, and especially by his mother. This is why he had resisted her efforts to contact him just before her death. It was only after William wrote him an extended letter filling in a lot of blanks about what really happened thirty years ago that he agreed to a reunion of the family in Terre Haute, Indiana, the year after his mother's death. His mother's prayer, although it was not answered in the way she would have liked while living, would be answered. Her sons would come to know each other. She had loved them unconditionally, and now they would have the opportunity to love one another. William knew in his heart that it was all because of Mother's prayer.

Chapter 2

৯৩৪৫

The Watsons

"Frances, come with me, this is something you'll want to see." This was a mild surprise to Frances, as everything was already so perfect that the word "want" wasn't a part of her vocabulary. The warmth, the peace, the music, the glow that touched everything did not leave a desire for more, yet the Angel repeated, "Frances, come see this." As she turned to the voice, a larger than life picture unfolded before her that immediately raised praise to her lips. There before her was a scene larger than anything she had ever witnessed in life. Displayed was the one thing her heart had yearned for most on earth. Her eyes misted as she took it all in. Heaven is wonderful, and now to see this too. "Quickly," she said, "summon the others. They'll want to be here. They'll want to see this." Tears flowed from her eyes as she viewed the scene before her. Soon others gathered by her side. Standing with her was her mother and father and her children Art, Orvie, and Ursie. Together they held hands as they watched the scene unfold before them. Frances spoke. "The one on

5

the left is Leo. Orvie and Ursie that's you brother. You didn't know him Orvie, but Ursie, you might remember him. I'd know him anywhere even though he was just eleven when I lost him. That must be his wife standing next to him. The fact that he's with the rest of my boys tells me he knows the whole story now. He always felt that I had deserted him and didn't care for him. Now he knows the true story. You children remember all I told you about your brothers, don't you? Well, there they all are. That handsome one in the middle in a uniform is Teddy with his bride Joyce. Don't you see the strong resemblance to Art? You're like two peas in a pod, I'd say. There on the right is Eddie, my last born with his wife Barbara. I told him about all of you and how he would have loved to have known you. He had to grow up without any brothers. He has such a good heart. Grandma and Granddad can testify to that. He's really the only one who truly got to know his grandparents well.

"I don't see any of the grandchildren around at this time; maybe they'll show up later. Ursie, what do you think of all of those brothers? Do you remember how some of them spoiled you? Orvie, these are all your younger siblings. My prayers are that you'll be reunited with them one day and can get to know them. That will be a wonderful celebration. I didn't get the opportunity to tell all of you on earth, but some may remember the words. If we never meet again this side of Heaven, we shall meet on that beautiful shore. This is our first complete family meeting, and I look forward to many, many more. Angel, thank you for setting all of this up for us."

"Will, Will, wake up. What are you doing, dreaming? You'd better shake a leg if you want to be on the road by ten." William didn't want to open his eyes; he wanted the dream to go on and on. He felt like he must be smiling. He felt so warm and loved and wanted to sleep again.

"Please let me sleep," he said, but it was too late. Molly had already brought him back to reality. He, Molly, and the kids would be driving to Terre Haute today to see Mrs. Newman and prepare for the reunion tomorrow with the brothers. The Trapp brothers, the four living Trapp brothers, would be together for the first time ever. What a red-letter day. He couldn't resist closing his eyes once again in an attempt to catch another glimpse of that dream he had just left. What a marvelous dream, Momma Trapp, Grandma and Granddad, Art, and little Ursie and Orvie. How fortunate he had been to be reunited with his mother and grandparents before their deaths. The picture didn't come again, so he kicked his legs over the side of the bed and sat up reaching for Molly as she passed by. Tears glazed his eyes as he tried to explain his dream and what she had interrupted by awakening him.

Molly stepped out of his reach and said, "We've got two hungry kids downstairs already and I'm sure they are bugging their grandparents to death, so I'd better go down there and fix their breakfast. We'll be in the car several hours today and that'll give you ample time to explain what I interrupted. Now I need to rescue your mother and father."

William sighed. He could only hope that was one dream that would replay again in the future. He sure wanted it to. As he showered and dressed he could hear the sounds and smell the aroma coming up the staircase. Nostalgic memories swept over him as he thought of the wonderful years he had spent in his parents' old twelve-room house in Webster Groves, Missouri. It had been totally remodeled in recent years, but it had not lost any of the feel that it had in his youth. Slightly overshadowing this nostalgia was the feeling that this era was coming to a close. The opportunities for visits were limited and his parents were not getting any younger. His father would be eighty-six this year and both he and William's mother had serious health issues. That's what prompted William to fly out with his family five days ago to spend time with them from their home in Falls Church, Virginia, where he ministered. How many more times would he have this chance? His kids, little Ursey, age 4, and Art, age 2, may never remember these wonderful people and that added to William's sadness as he dressed. He would do everything he could so they would remember. Art, his son, was named Charles Arthur Watson. He was named for his grandfather and for his uncle who had died in the war. Arthur was the war hero and brother who had saved William's life. When his children were older they would certainly know the story and circumstances of when Art had saved their daddy's life. Ursey's name also had family connections that she would one day also understand. He tied his shoes and got up. He wasn't wanting to think further about that day coming too soon when this wonderful sanctuary and these wonderful, warm people would no longer be available to touch and feel. God had truly blessed him the day these parents selected him as their son at the orphanage.

He descended the stairway and headed for the kitchen where everyone had chosen to gather on this frosty morning. The sight and aromas that met his senses brightened his day. The love and happiness apparent before him hung in the air like a lovely cloud. What a blessing to see them all together. His dad was busy pouring milk in the kid's glasses, and they were all trying to talk at once. What a lovely noise.

After lingering over breakfast, and his parents telling the children many stories of his antics as a child, it was time to pack up and hit the road in their rented vehicle. William told Molly just the night before; "You know it was just eight months ago that we made the trip to Charleston for Mom's funeral. It seems a lot has happened since then." Molly agreed. She felt they had been most fortunate to have known Frances and spend time with her before her death. Getting to know his grandparents, Uncle Willis, Aunt Lou, and others had meant so much to him. Frances deserved so much credit for the man this husband of hers had become, as well as what she had instilled in her own first love, Arthur. These brothers that had blessed her life had so many things in common, and so many of their values had come from Frances.

Charles Jr., whom everyone called AJ, stopped by after breakfast to say goodbye. AJ's mother decided soon after his birth that she wanted to avoid the confusion of too many Charles in the house so she dubbed him AJ then and there. After all he was "A Junior," so she just called him AJ. It stuck, and all his life family and friends had called him AJ. William loved his big brother. Though he was twenty years William's senior, and they had never actually lived under the same roof, AJ's acceptance of him thirty years ago when his parents brought him home was total. AJ was his parent's child. Too bad they couldn't have had a couple of dozen kids like him. The world would be the better for it. His children were almost as old as William and they were like brothers to him. AJ had taken over his father's successful business and ran it with the same success and integrity that his father had. He had patterned his life after Charles and Kathryn Watson. He couldn't go wrong.

William said, "I'll be looking for you in the fall out east. You're long overdue for a visit and I'm holding you to it."

AJ said. "I wouldn't miss it for the world. You can show the family the great state of Virginia. Are they still fighting the war down there? I keep on hearing the South is going to rise again."

William had a private conversation with his brother and asked him to please call if there was any change in his parents' health at any time. AJ asked that William consider relocating back to the Midwest where they could see him more often. "It would mean a lot to all of us," he said. There were hugs all around and the William Watson family loaded up and headed east across the Mississippi, destination Indiana. William had made the trip many times over the years.

Chapter 3

ৡৡঌ

The Trapps

Lloyd Edward Trapp, nicknamed Eddie, had already been on the road six hours and still wasn't out of the state of Kansas. He had left home in Cheyenne Wells, Colorado, early in the morning and had fought Kansas' crosswinds and sagebrush all morning along Route 36. The further east he got, the less sagebrush. In a way, it all helped him stay alert driving alone. The plans to meet the brothers in Terre Haute so soon after having attended his mom's funeral in Charleston were unexpected. He and his wife had discussed it and decided that it wasn't very practical for both of them to pack the kids up and leave their struggling business again this soon. As much as Barbara would have liked to get better acquainted, finances and obligations dictated that one of them stay at home. For three years now they had been struggling with making their small restaurant, bar, and pool room combination successful in Cheyenne Wells. It was a small town, but Barbara's family was well-known, and through hard work they were paying the bills and satisfying the bank on the mortgage. It took long hours and dedication with both of them working, but some of Barb's family would temporarily step up and help out in his absence. His part would be to economize on the trip, and he did so by carrying food with him and planning not to stop at hotels along the way. He figured the thousand-mile trip would take about twenty-four hours including stops for rest and gas, and he had good reliable transportation, so he didn't anticipate any extra expense or trouble. It would be a long twenty-four hours with just his radio and his thoughts, but he had a lot to think about. He was finally going to meet Leo.

His first trip across Kansas wasn't quite this easy back in the late forties. He and his high school friend George had set out to work their way west by following the wheat harvest. Crossing the state of Kansas took the biggest part of a hot July. It was tough leaving his mother so soon after graduating from high school in Oakland, Illinois, and he knew he must have broken her heart. At the time he really felt it was necessary. The first eighteen years of his life had been a mixed bag. He had to get away and be his own man, if he ever wanted to be a useful man. Part of it was adventure, but part was the result of some painful experiences that he never shared with a soul until he met and married Barbara in Colorado. She's the only one that knows the whole story of what Eddie had grown up with. Despite Momma's love and nurturing, there were aspects of his life that he couldn't share with her. In hindsight, it was the right move for him and the fact that he had a loving wife and two children now is justification for what he did. He still has a way to go, but he's a better man for striking out on his own. He'd found a wonderful family when he had married Barbara and had gotten to know her parents and siblings.

Somewhere in mid-Missouri he pulled off the highway for a rest. The temperature was mild so he just locked the doors and bundled up in a blanket and spread out the best he could. He awoke about five hours later, not especially refreshed, but enough so that he knew he could complete the trip without getting sleepy at the wheel. He would be in Terre Haute by early morning, get another nap, freshen up, and then join his brothers and families at the designated meeting place for lunch. The closer he got, the more excited he was becoming.

He had been surprised about three months ago when William had called from his home in Virginia telling him that he had made contact with Leo, the brother that was not at Mom's funeral. From notes that his mother had left in the Bible, William had contacted Leo and the end result was that Leo wanted very much to meet with all of his brothers. Was Eddie interested? Of course he was, he couldn't wait! William asked for his ideas and then talked with the others about the time and place. They had selected Terre Haute. It was the most central, but mainly it was where their brother Art was buried. It wasn't that far from Coles County, Illinois, where they all had been born, in case some of them wanted to revisit their past. Eddie had thoughts of all of them and wanted to know more about them. That's what this reunion was all about. Their time spent together at Moms in the fifties and then at her death had been minimal, but he treasured the time he had with them. Eddie was born after the others had already been taken to the Children's Home. They had never lived together.

Eddie was thinking that God had a reason for providing this family with a William. He was special. Eddie had wanted to name his son after William but went with Rudy instead.

That was Barb's younger brother's name. Eddie couldn't help but wonder how different his life would have been had he grown up with his brothers in a stable home environment. It had meant so much to him to learn of the circumstances of his brothers' lives. Wonderful parents had chosen them all and things had turned out so well in that regard. In Eddie's mind, his mom's prayers had a lot to do with that. He could still remember hearing her prayers through the thin walls at the Knights, sometimes late at night when she couldn't sleep. He always felt protected when his mom was praying.

His Uncle Willis' persevered in the search, with others' help, and now William's efforts had brought the search to a conclusion. William, the army chaplain of World War II, the ordained minister of the cloth, the brother who took the information and ran with it by first drawing Teddy back into the fold, and now Leo. If only his mom had survived long enough to have been there tomorrow with them. He was so looking forward to getting to know all of them better and being a part of an extended family once again. It had been a long time. For a while he had felt like the outsider, but that didn't last long. They were flesh and blood and the fit was soon made. After all, he was the one who knew their mom the best, and this whole relationship keyed around their wonderful mom.

In the back of Eddie's mind was also the plan to stop at Uncle Willis' on the way back for a visit. We all owe that man a lot, he thought. On other visits, Eddie could sense that Willis felt some guilt for not doing more to keep the family together in the first place. Discussions that Eddie had with William and Ted clearly exonerated Willis. No one could fully understand the circumstances of the family in the depression years, an ill woman deserted by a husband,

and Willis' subsequent efforts, but the brothers believed the man had done all that was possible. It was questionable that Granddad McGrew did what he should have done, but Momma had clearly forgiven him and that was the end of that.

He had passed the sign some miles back that said Charleston so he knew he'd be approaching the Wabash River before long. Crossing over the Wabash River was not as impressive as crossing the Mississippi, but it was the end of the trail and he was ready for that. With a little sleep and a nice clean station restroom to freshen up in, he'd be ready for the big event.

Chapter 4

❧❧

The Swensons

Leo Swenson considered himself a pragmatic man. No one had accused him of being a warm and fuzzy person or one who was likely to get overly excited or alarmed about anything. That had helped him the six years he spent in the Navy, four during the war. He didn't develop his personality there, however, as it was already in place as a result of his early upbringing. He was the oldest of four boys living at the poverty level, with a father who rarely bothered to speak to him, let alone love, nurture, or even discipline him. His momma did all of these things, but it affects a boy when he doesn't feel he's important to his father. It's best to cover up the emotion and toughen oneself and pretend it doesn't matter. He was his momma's helper and his siblings' protector, but one day that went away and his childhood was lost forever. He remembered beautiful little sick Ursie, but she wasn't with them long. While she was there, she got all of Daddy's attention and love. Sometimes Leo resented that. Not Ursie, but the father who didn't pass love around and share it with the boys. But one day that all changed. His last reminder from his mom was to look after his younger brothers and he didn't get that done, so the shell he built around himself became harder. When the Swensons adopted him he was sure that life was only going to be rougher. The early years with his adopted parents didn't do much to salve his wounds either. Later on he understood, but a pre-teenager didn't know that these new parents, new from the old country with no child raising experiences, were struggling to adjust also. It was a long time before he didn't feel like he was being exploited for his labor. He was wrong, but it took time and the skin got tougher. The one person in the world who loved him had given him away.

No doubt, he was pragmatic. Some would say stubborn, unyielding, or even systematic. He tended to keep his guard up with everyone, except his family. He had no reservations when it came to his wife Carol and their son and daughter. He did hold back on the contents of the letter he received from his long lost brother William. His wife knew he received it, but he asked her to give him some time before he'd be ready to talk about it. It was, of course, the letter that William sent after the death of Frances explaining in much detail all that he knew about what had happened thirty years ago when the four boys were put up for adoption in the Children's Home. It also had about a page each on the brothers that he'd been separated from and what was happening in their lives. He was saddened when he read of Arthur's death during the war. Even with all this, he was not immediately moved to rejoice, or show remorse for not being receptive to his birth mother when she tried to contact him last year. He had closed the door on those memories many years ago and it was difficult to open it again. As he absorbed all this he wasn't convinced that he wanted to shake the status quo. His children were not even aware he had been adopted and this was taking a chance that his parents might be hurt too, by reopening this book that had been closed so long.

The betrayal by his father, and then his mother, was partially explained in the letter he received. He thought about that fateful call from a cousin last year that had tried to connect with him, but he wasn't ready. He really didn't want to think his momma had given him up easily, and now it was clear she was only looking after the boy's welfare. She truly thought she was on her deathbed. Of course, there was no redeeming information that changed what he felt for his natural father. The only thing William said was that he was alive and apparently well. He did remember to pray about it. Sometimes prayer was the only peace he could find in difficult times. It had sure helped him survive the war.

He put a lot of thought into the process of deciding what he should do. He became more sensitive to the children, their attitudes, personalities and interests. He was trying to find a clue of how they would react. Katie had a lively, sparkling personality, much like his wife Carol, but he noted his son was at times a brooder, and he wondered how much his own actions contributed to that. His son William, who was named after his brother who was now contacting him, appeared to have several of his own personality traits, and some of them weren't that attractive. It was an awakening to him and he began to think of ways he could change to be a better role model. Maybe forgiveness and opening himself to the uncertain and unknown could be a step in the right direction.

It was a school night, and as soon as the kids were tucked in bed he asked Carol to join him on the sofa in the living room. He said, "I'm ready to talk about the letter and I want you to read it through for yourself. You have always let me know you supported my decisions in this matter and I think it's time to talk about making some changes." The reading and discussion went on for a couple of hours until, exhausted, they agreed to sleep on it. The next day they were of one mind and Leo called his parents in Mendota to make plans for a weekend get-together. The die was cast. The Swensons were very understanding. They had never hinted that Carol and Leo should withhold anything from the children. That had been Leo's decision and now he should definitely do as his heart led him. They'd do anything they could do to help.

Weeks later Carol and Leo were motoring south on Route 51 to avoid going through Chicago on their way to Indiana. They didn't often have a chance to be alone and they made the best of it. The grandparents came to Rockford to baby-sit the children, and although the kids put up a fuss for not being included, the plans had been made weeks ago and they recognized their arguments were not going to win. All they were told was that Mom and Dad were meeting some old friends down in Indiana for a couple of days.

Anticipation for this day had grown on Leo, and now it had loosened his tongue more than Carol had ever witnessed. She laughed at him and kidded that he was giving her a day-by-day history of his early childhood, if not a minute-by-minute one. She laughed with him, as many were good memories he had not previously shared. The shadows were lifting. She prayed that only positive things would come out of this and the darker moments would take a backseat forever. It felt good. She was most fortunate to have found this good man.

Chapter 5

❧❧

The Wainrights

Ted and Joyce Wainright had established a home in Alexandria, Virginia after their marriage. Ted had been assigned to the Pentagon at the time and it was conveniently close to Joyce's parents, who were retired military. Joyce didn't have much problem adjusting to military life. That was all she ever knew. Over the years, as Ted was posted to various places in Europe and around the states, they maintained their home in Alexandria. It was a modest home, but it was theirs. When they were assigned elsewhere, they lived in military housing.

One advantage of maintaining their base in Alexandria was that they were relatively close to William, Ted's brother. Joyce thought it was wonderful how the two had bonded. Since Ted had grown up as an only child, the discovery of family was a major happening in his life. William had an older brother, AJ, but up until that day eight or nine years ago when they met, Ted's entire family was just his mother and father. Joyce and Ted and their children spent quality time with the Watson family when they were living in the area. They made it a practice to get together at least once a month and their children had grown close. They found they had much in common. The fact that William was a minister didn't get in the way. Ted was very comfortable with that.

It was at one of the family get-togethers that William filled them in on the contact he had made with their older brother Leo. William was working on a plan for a reunion of the Trapp family. He wanted to get all four of the sons of Frances Trapp still living to one place at one time. Molly and William were very excited by the idea and the plans were going forward. Privately, Ted was less than enthusiastic. At times it appeared the reconnection with William was enough for Ted, and while he and Joyce did make a couple of trips to Illinois over the years to see Frances while she was still alive, he never had the fervor that William had about meeting the others. Joyce surmised that Ted was just so young, five at the time when the Wainrights adopted him, and he had little or no memory of them. On the other hand, he had a wonderful relationship with his own father and mother and they were just a few hours away at the Virginia Military Institute where his father was still Commandant.

Ted was thinking of the impending plans for going to Indiana the next week for the reunion. It wasn't that he was disinterested in meeting Leo; it just wasn't a high priority after all these years. Traveling a thousand miles with his family for two days was a major commitment. He considered canceling, using his mother's illness as an excuse, but sensed she wouldn't approve of that.

"Do what you want to do," she would say, "but don't use me for a crutch Theodore."

Ted was so concerned for her. Though not yet seventy, her heart was weakening quickly. Her family didn't have a good track record in that regard and all of the best medical care in the world wasn't helping. His father had already given notice he would be resigning at the end of the current academic year so that he could take her south to a warmer climate. The old mansion they lived in was beautiful, but it was drafty and the heating wasn't adequate. No, he suspected his mother would want him to make the trip. He punched the intercom button and told his secretary to make flight reservations for the four of them to Indianapolis. Joyce had not forced the issue with Ted, but he knew his wife. As an only child herself, she was enthralled with the idea of an extended family and all the possibilities that it held. Also, he had to do it for William. He would never want to disappoint him. William and his family had already left as they were planning to visit family in Missouri for a few days.

There was a message in Ted's in basket when he returned from lunch. It was from his old roommate and friend from West Point, Joe Brown. He and his wife would be in Washington, D.C., the first of April and wanted to make plans to get together. He noted the message said "Colonel Brown," which Ted knew was Joe's way of telling him he had finally caught up with him in rank. Their paths had not crossed much since Ted was the best man at Joe and Donna's wedding. Joe had been in Ted's wedding six months later, but the Army put a lot of distance between them since then. Most of Ted's duty tended toward the European continent. Joe had several tours to the Pacific area since his first involvement in Korea years ago. They stayed in touch and the old competitiveness that began at the Point years ago was still there. Joe graduated at the top of their class and as it turned out, Joe married the girl that Ted had courted for four years. But, that turned out okay. Donna, Joe's wife was a jewel, but his Joyce was an heirloom. With Donna he would have had a show wife that would have fostered his career, but with Joyce he had a wife and mother who made a home first, wherever they were.

Chapter 6

࿇

Mrs. Newman

Being much more familiar with the city, Molly directed William where to turn to get to the Newman home in Terre Haute. William had been there several times, but places change over the years. This had been Molly's second home for years. She and Art Newman were dating before Art went into the service. Even after Art's death, she was a constant visitor to the Newman home and loved the family dearly. They had lost their son, but Molly was still like a daughter to them. They corresponded frequently. She had flown back two years ago when Mr. Newman had died. William was incapacitated from a water skiing accident and couldn't come, but she wanted to be there for Mrs. Newman. Mrs. Newman, or Beth as they now called her, was so looking forward to their coming and insisted they stay at her place. "I'm counting on you to be here in time for dinner," she had said.

Molly wasn't from Terre Haute originally. She'd only taken her nurse's training here and worked in the local hospital. That's where she was when she met a young orderly, Arthur

25

Newman, and fell in love. She was from a town across the state line, Paris, Illinois, but she didn't have family there anymore. They had all died or had moved away. George and Elizabeth Newman had been her parents in a real sense of the word after Arthur was killed. She thought she would probably live out her life without another true love, but she was wrong. William Watson had shown up after the war, and while there was an immediate connection to this wonderful man, it was years before their affection grew into a deep and abiding love. They were separated by hundreds of miles, but something kept drawing them back together. When they married, the only ones happier than the Newmans had been the bride and groom themselves. William had become special to them also.

As they pulled into the driveway, Beth with her apron flapping in the wind came out to greet them. What a warm reunion it was. They quickly herded her and the children inside. The March air was just a little too nippy for a housedress. As Beth patted the children's heads and took off their sweaters, her hugs and kisses may have overwhelmed them a little. Molly only smiled and knew they would survive it.

Talk was at a mile a minute through dinner and afterwards about every aspect of their lives. The kids entertained themselves for a while as the adults lingered over coffee and dessert. Though they had been here after Frances' funeral, they had been rushed and now had a lot of catching up to do. At bedtime, Beth tucked the children in as William helped Molly in the kitchen. After that, they sat down and discussed the events of the following day. "Beth, I want to thank you for making all the arrangements for tomorrow," William said. "The place sounds perfect and the chance of having a comfortable meeting place away from the attention of the other restaurant patrons is wonderful. We're fortunate your brother has such a place and we insist on reimbursing him for his trouble."

Beth said, "No, he won't take any payment except for the food you eat, and the hall is yours for as long as you want it." They sat and talked quietly and reminisced until the yawning started. The timetable for leaving the restaurant and going to the cemetery where Art was buried alongside his father was decided on and they prepared to turn in. Beth had told them that others had asked to attend but she informed them that this was a special memorial time for Art's brothers and she'd asked them not to come. They had understood.

Despite the events ahead, that household slept peacefully and soundly that night. Another couple, Leo and Carol were also sleeping in a motel not too far from them, although Leo was keyed up and had a restless night. Joyce and Ted were sleeping soundly in their own bed, but would be rising early to catch the plane. They should arrive on time for lunch unless the plane was delayed. They'd drive to Terre Haute from Indianapolis, a trip of about fifty miles. It shouldn't be too rough on the children.

Chapter 7

❧

The Reunion

Eddie was feeling pretty good after sleeping six hours, a decent breakfast, a change of clothes and a shave. He was running a little early when he got to the restaurant so he stopped at the coffee shop section and waited for the others to arrive. He was making small talk with the waiter when he saw William arrive with his family and Mrs. Newman. He greeted them at the front door with hugs and an older gentlemen led them to the back of the restaurant where a private room was set up for them. William introduced the older gentleman as the owner of the restaurant and Mrs. Newman's brother who had so graciously supplied the room for the day. In the few minutes before the others started to arrive, Eddie was getting acquainted with the children and telling them about his two children who couldn't make it today. He'd previously told William over the phone that he would be making the trip alone.

"Eddie, would you have time to show us around Charleston and Coles County? You grew up there," William had asked.

"I'd like that," he had replied.

At one end of the room three round tables had been pushed together forming a diamond shaped arrangement. At the other end were four upholstered chairs and two sofas with various end tables and lamps along with a coffee table. Along one wall was a lengthy table complete with coffee maker, drinks, glasses, cups, and ice. "We're expecting fourteen," William said. "I'm not sure whether Uncle Willis and Aunt Lou will be here for lunch or not. They said they would try." That was good news to Eddie. He was looking forward to visiting with them. Uncle Willis, his mom's brother, was about the only relative other than Grandmother and Granddad that Eddie knew growing up.

The next couple arriving were Leo and his wife Carol. Although William had not seen this brother in over thirty years, there was no mistaking who he was. As their eyes locked, they came together in a big hug, and then holding each other at arms length they studied each other's faces for what seemed like minutes. Eyes glistened all around and finally the silence was broken when Leo said, "I see you grew up," as he peered up at the taller brother, "I used to look down on you." This brought laughter to the room, as William was clearly six inches taller than Leo. William quickly made introductions to the others present. Eddie and Leo stood toe-to-toe and Leo said to him, "At least you're the right height, you didn't outgrow me." As all of them stood arms entwined, Eddie explained why his family wasn't present and how his wife Barbara so looked forward to meeting Leo and Carol. Leo told them their children were with Leo's parents. This was all so new and they needed more time before they tried to explain it all to them. "They have never known that I was adopted," Leo volunteered.

Ted, Joyce and children were the next to walk in with Uncle Willis and Aunt Lou. They had met in the parking lot. Eddie half expected to see Ted in uniform, but Ted didn't normally travel in uniform when his family was along. After Ted and Leo shook hands and had time to size each other up, Ted introduced him to Joyce. There were warm greetings all around. Ted had felt an unusual emotion when he saw his brothers. An emotion he had not expected. It brought a lump to his throat that he swallowed hard to cover up. He had seen death on the battlefield and had been in many serious situations, but this sensation was one he didn't know. His normal professional reserve melted quickly as he hugged each of them again in turn and told them how very happy he was to finally see them all together. Joyce couldn't help but smile as she read his emotional state and was deeply touched. This made the trip worthwhile. Seeing these four brothers together for the first time ever was a sight she would never forget. They all seemed so natural and comfortable together.

After a time of sharing, William asked if anyone was hungry or ready to eat. The kids let him know that they were. It was decided that the four children should have their own table as they knew each other and wished to show their independence. A table was brought in and set up next to the adult tables and the four of them, Ursey, James, Charles, and Casey were ready to be served. Waiters took everyone's luncheon order, and as they waited William offered a prayer of thanksgiving for the food and for the family assembled.

"One thing I remember," Leo said after the prayer, "was that Mom would often say the prayer and then ask each of us what we were thankful for."

"I'd almost forgotten that," William said, "but you're right. In fact, I remember one thing you were thankful for

Leo, and that was the teeter-totters at school. I also know why you liked them. Remember how you used to buck them and toss me off the other end. You were like a bronco rider."

"I got bucked off plenty of times myself," Leo responded. They all laughed at this exchange. "I remember that Teddy was always thankful for cherry pie," Leo said. "Mom would say, but Teddy we don't have cherry pie today, but that didn't matter, he was still thankful for cherry pie."

"I think he knew what he was doing, though," William said, "because normally within a day or two Mom would bake a pie when she could."

Joyce spoke up and said, "Some things never change."

Mrs. Newman quietly said, "That explains something to me that was so endearing but something I never fully understood. Art, when he was growing up, would quite often repeat the same thing after our family prayer in the evening. He'd say, thank God for my warm bed and blankets. I understand now where he learned that." Things were just a little quieter for a moment as each of them thought of the missing brother. They continued to reminisce as the food came and as they ate.

Eddie was reminded that one of his favorite memories of growing up was of Mom's homemade bread and its wonderful aroma. "She'd cut it while it was hot and sneak me a buttered piece before dinner time. In fact, the last time I visited her, before she got to sick too cook, she made bread and a cherry pie for me." The others remembered her bread also.

"Sometimes when we didn't have much else," Leo said, "if Mom had flour and yeast she'd make bread and we always had milk from the cow."

The small talk continued throughout lunch with very few interruptions to referee or help out at the children's table.

The ladies were exchanging stories about their husbands and themselves. Joyce and Carol had so much in common with their Irish ancestry and all of them just loved Joyce's red hair. They were both descendants of the immigrants of the great Irish potato famine of the 1800's and the ladies told of the tough beginnings their parents had experienced.

Toward the end of the meal Ted addressed his Uncle Willis. "I know you played a major part in what's happening today, and I for one would like to hear just how you tracked us all down and how long you worked at it. That trail must have turned cold a long time ago, and yet for over twenty years you pursued it. What kept you going?"

Willis slowly pushed back from the table. "As usual, I've eaten too much. At home I'd have to have a nap break." He paused a moment before he started in. "First, let me say I feel a little sheepish for getting that much credit. I've always carried guilt around because it had to happen in the first place. The fact that you boys were given up for adoption is a disgrace to my family, and I wish we had those years to live over again. I was in my twenties at the time and struggling myself, but something should have been done. Secondly, let me emphasize that it was your mother's perseverance and prayer that made me want to contribute to the search. She didn't have any resources, except for a few family members, but she continually pressed them, one on one, for ideas and thoughts. It was her burning commitment that made me want to help when I got in the position where I could. When the first clue fell into my lap right here in Terre Haute, I didn't know what to do. I literally sat on that news, at least in part, for years, not wanting to create problems, but also not knowing what the entire situation involved. Some of you have never had the opportunity to meet my Uncle Adren or remember him, but he was a true friend and ally to your mom. He pushed the search idea whenever he could. I remember how angry he got with his brother Jesse who had run across information on Leo and failed to pass it on for over four years. He did what he could to help keep Frances' spirits up, and when necessary he'd remind her that she also had to consider each of you and your welfare. He's like a brother to me. In fact, he's a couple of years younger than me. Your Grandmother McGrew, my mother, was twenty-six years older than he was. I still get to see him three or four times a year. To my knowledge, the only time your mom used bad judgment with the information she received was when she called Leo without properly assessing the situation or getting the input from the rest of us. Leo, she was very ill at the time and I hope you've forgiven that."

Leo spoke up. "I do understand."

Willis went on with a narrative of events for nearly a half hour, filling the men in on everything he could remember that he thought might be of interest. All of them listened intently. Of special interest to them was the story that it was William's parents who had directed Ted's parents, complete strangers, to the Children's Home. "I owe a lot to my daughter-in-law for that one," he said. "I was ready to give up the search." At the end he said, "I want to thank God on behalf of myself and my dear sister for watching over each of you. God had a plan for your lives and I am so proud of each of you and what you have become. Mr. Kirkley at the Children's Home may have rushed to judgment and given you all up for adoption too soon. In hindsight though, if your mother had died, as everyone thought she would, the adoptions were the right thing at the time. Each of you has been blessed with wonderful, caring families. My regrets are that it took so long for you to get back together, and of course, that your mom isn't here. She had such faith though, and I know she knows. Thank you for including Lou and me in your reunion. I just want you to know it's one of the biggest honors I have ever had, and one of my happier moments in life to see you all here. I know that others are smiling down on this day also. I'm going to shut up now and head for one of those couches over there. I need a short nap." They all chuckled. "I'll take questions later. Don't forget what your brother William did. He put together a major piece of the puzzle. I hope one day I'll have the chance to meet all of your parents and families. It would be a great honor to thank them also. You know, back in 1918 the Whitfords started an annual reunion that still meets the fourth Sunday in August in Paris, Illinois. My grandfather and his brothers started it. I'd love to introduce each of you to your extended family. There's still a sizeable clan around. Uncle Adren has eight kids himself. If you're ever going to be in the area in August, be sure and call me so we can go over there.

After lunch the kids played, and the cameras came out for individual and group pictures. No one had forgotten to bring one. Everyone exchanged phone numbers and addresses. After everyone was exhausted of picture taking, the ladies claimed the sofas and chairs along with Willis, and the men gathered with their coffee over to one side. They delved in depth into the lives of each other and shared many things. Leo, Ted, and William had the war years in common, but Eddie listened intently to anything and everything they had to say. In return, they wanted to know all he could tell about the eighteen years that he and his mom had spent with the Knight family. He relayed the story to Leo of how their mother had ended up with the Knight family, and although

Ted and William had heard it from her own lips, they were interested in Eddie's version once again. They also wanted to know of Eddie's hopes and aspirations. He was the youngest of the clan, being five years younger than Teddy, and they quickly became older brothers deeply interested in his life and welfare. That meant so much to Eddie to experience this exchange and the bonding that was so obviously taking place. It filled a large void in his life.

They were also rehashing their deep dark secrets of their childhood in Canaan. William reminded Leo of the neighbor's buggy and he laughed. For the others he said, "It was Leo's idea. Mrs. Edmond would on occasion watch us when Mom needed to go someplace. She had an old buggy down by her barn that no one ever used. It was for a single horse and Leo got the idea that we could back it down the hill by the barn until it would almost get away from us, and then pull it back. We'd done that several times, marking our spot each time and trying to go further the next. Leo and Ted would be on one side and Art and I on the other. We'd almost surpassed our best mark when Ted slipped and tripped Leo and they went down losing their grip and the buggy started down the hill. I yelled for Art to let go and sat down and the buggy picked up speed. The wheels got turned on a rock or something and the buggy flipped, sending Art, who was still holding on, flying into the air. The height he flew has increased over time in my memory, but it seemed he went ten feet into the air and lit on his feet at the bottom before falling on his bottom. The wagon ended up twisted at the bottom with Art nearby. He got up, dusted his britches and said, 'Hey, somebody let go'. We were all so stunned that it was a minute or two before we could think to do anything. There was no way we could get the buggy back up the hill so we just decided to leave it there and not say anything. It didn't look broken or anything. Surprisingly, nothing was ever mentioned about that buggy to Mom and we made Art promise not to tell. He didn't. That was typical of Art. He was loyal and he would never give up."

Mrs. Newman had heard the start of the story and had joined them to listen. She said, "He never changed. I remember when he started high school he wanted so much to play football, but because he wasn't yet a hundred pounds we didn't think he should. He became a freshman manager, however, and the coaches really learned to appreciate his efforts. When the second year came around, although he was still the smallest guy on the squad, they let him play. About the second week of practice they jumped on the back of a truck to ride back to the school from the ball field and he was accidentally pushed off at a curve, hitting his head and causing a concussion. He was ready to go back the next week but the doctor said no. From then on the coaches convinced him to be equipment manager and they told us he was the best they'd ever had. He didn't quit, and he never did." Tears glistened in everyone's eyes as she shared the story.

Leo asked Ted if he remembered William trying to burn down the woods, and Ted said no. "Well fellows, your brother William was no saint. Don't let his mild manners deceive you. He had a thing with matches and liked to light fires, but of course not when Mom was around. I was near the garden one day when I saw a curl of smoke coming out the woods near the creek. About that time here comes Teddy running as fast as his little short legs would carry him. I asked him what was wrong and all he could say was, 'Billy's started a big fire.' I grabbed a bucket from the well and headed that way and found William trying to splash water out of the creek onto the spreading fire near the shoreline. I jumped into the creek and started using the bucket to throw water on the fire until it was out, and got soaked in the process. About that time Mom showed up and I got scolded for getting my clothes all wet. She didn't say anything to William except to ask what he was doing. He explained that he had been trying to start a little campfire for him and Teddy. They were making camp here, but I had come and put out the fire. I quickly defended myself by saying he was trying to burn down the woods, but Momma only told him not to mess around with matches anymore. He said he wouldn't. Going back to the house he told me under his breath where Mom couldn't hear him, 'I had everything taken care of and besides everything was still damp from a recent rain. Besides that, the woods are too big, they needed thinned out.' To his credit though, he didn't try any more camp fires down by the woods."

William said, "I'd had a beautiful camp fire too, if the wind hadn't started blowing."

Ted was curious about Eddie's nose. The McGrew family nose that he and Eddie both had was small to start with, but Eddie's had obviously been badly broken and not properly set. Eddie just said, "that's a sadder tale for another day. Let's just say it didn't do much for my looks and I was never a boxer." He in turn asked Ted about his friendship with Audie Murphy. "I'm a big fan of his. Every since you told me about him, I've seen everything he ever did in the movies. Some were good and some not so good. Do you still hear from him from time to time?"

"I do," Ted said. "In fact, we're due to go bird hunting some time this year. He has a home down in Georgia with major acreage and I've been there to hunt before. He admits some of his movies have been duds, but he has a contract with the studio and has to pretty much do the ones they want him too. He's still a wonderful guy though. Hollywood hasn't changed him all that much and I look forward to catching up to him this year to renew our friendship." Leo wasn't familiar with the name until Ted explained that Audie was the most decorated American soldier in World War II. Ted had met him while a student at West Point. This prompted a few war stories from Leo. They were especially interested in his first person's account of December 7, 1941 at Pearl Harbor.

This conversation went on non-stop with no posturing or reservations at all. It was like they had been together everyday of their lives, and the give and take was all in fun as they just understood each other so well. They were amazed themselves and finally Eddie put it into words. "This proves that blood is thicker than water. Who else could go from being virtual strangers to best friends in a few short hours."

Ted and William told Leo the story of their first meeting with their mom. William said, "Leo, you probably remember our young mom better than the rest of us. She never lost that special warmth and sweet smile. The years were tough ones, but she held tight to her love of God and family. She got so ill in the end and, in a way, I suspect she probably would rather you remember her the way she was."

Leo questioned them at length on all they could remember about their mother and about Art. "The little guy made us proud, didn't he?" was Leo's response.

In the meantime the ladies had covered the waterfront in their discussions. There wasn't anything that they hadn't talked about. Willis had gotten a short nap in and awoke in time to hear them talking about their children. As they watched the four present, playing so well together, Carol wished hers were here also. The ages of their children were from two to twelve. William, Carol's oldest, was twelve. Her daughter Kathleen, or Katie as she was called, was eight. As it so happened, each family had a boy and a girl. Willis told them about Eddie's children, Rudy and Debby. He was pretty sure they were six and eight. Molly told them Ursey was named after William's little sister that had died just the year before the family was separated. Ursey was almost five and Charles Arthur, her son, had just turned three. Joyce had the youngest with Casey who was just two and James Theodore who was six. James was named after his Grandfather Wainright.

Mrs. Newman was busy writing this all down as she wanted to remember names and birthdays. "Your children may want to know who that old lady is that keeps sending them cards on birthdays and holidays. Well, just tell them I'm a want-to-be aunt." Joyce had fallen in love with this woman Molly already claimed as a mother. Lou, Willis' wife, was sitting back and enjoying it all. It was wonderful to see this family grow together after all these years. She would never have visualized this happening ten years ago.

Time passed so quickly and before they realized it was three o'clock, the time they had set for going to the cemetery. They figured out their car-pools and headed out, noticeably quieter than they had been. William led the way. Thankfully they had decent weather because the Newman family plot wasn't along the roadways of the Vigo County Cemetery. The site was on a little knoll in a newer section, and the stones erected for Art and his father and mother were matching. Vase holders were attached to both and new spring flowers were in place that Mrs. Newman had delivered by the florist that very morning. Art's stone had an engraved American flag. They took a minute to explain to the children what they were seeing and the identity of their loved ones who had died and gone on to Heaven. Their bodies that they didn't need anymore were placed here. The whole family stood in silence for a minute.

Mrs. Newman spoke first. "I just want to say what this all means to me. Losing our son was such a tragedy in our lives, but getting to know all of you has been such a blessing. I wish George was here with us in person today, but I know he is in spirit. To those of you who I met twelve years ago and have grown to love, and to Art's family that I'm just beginning to know, I just want to say thank you for including me. You all feel like family to me and I just want to say God bless you all, because He certainly has blessed me. You remind me in so many ways of my son."

This triggered another round of hugs and tears. Then the women and children stepped over to one side as Art's brothers surrounded his stone holding hands. The oldest, Leo spoke first. "Let's join hands here over our fallen brother and honor him. Let's also honor our mother who never gave up on us." Leo continued to speak and then both Eddie and Ted said a few words also.

William was the last to speak that day at the gravesite. He opened with a prayer and then thanked God for all of this brothers and family assembled there. He thanked God for Mrs. Newman and in closing he said, "I feel we are where we are today because of Mother's prayer. She is at the core of each of us and much of the strength we have can be attributed to her prayers every day of her adult life." He concluded his talk with these words, "If we never meet again this side of Heaven, we will meet on that beautiful shore." These words had so much significance to each of them.

Leo had one concluding thought when he said, "Because of Mother's prayer."

With that they all huddled together for fully two minutes and then dispersed to their family and cars for the return trip to the restaurant. Dinner and more visiting was to follow, but the evening was cut short because the children were tiring and Ted's family had to make connections for their flight back to Virginia. Uncle Willis had convinced Eddie to come to Charleston that night to get a good rest before starting back to Colorado. Eddie, Leo and William would be meeting the next day to explore old haunts in Coles County. Eddie knew his way around and Leo wanted very much to revisit this place he had not seen in over thirty years. William and Molly had made plans to go to Paris in the morning so the kids could see where their mother was born and raised. William had never been there either and was eager to see the town that had nurtured his wife. So with pledges all around to make this reunion at least an annual affair and to keep in touch, the boys went their separate ways. Molly and William stayed overnight in Terre Haute with Mrs. Newman again. They were all in agreement. It had been a wonderful day.

Chapter 8

☙ ❧

Coles County

The Watsons went to Paris the next morning via the two-lane highway that Molly had traveled many times when she was a student in nursing in the thirties. She stayed in Terre Haute most of the time due to lack of transportation, but over a two-year period there were many trips. It was a short trip, less than twenty-five miles, and before they knew it they were on Main Street, downtown looking at the Courthouse. The Edgar County Courthouse was one of the more impressive buildings, as courthouses go, in towns of similar size in the Midwest, if not the nation. It sat in the expanse of several acres surrounded by grass and shrubbery with an eighteen-inch high concrete border fence that was rounded on top. On the east side, near where they parked, was the memorial to the fallen of Edgar County in all of the nation's wars. Molly explained how during the summer they had band concerts on the lawn and they could sit on the fence and listen or play in the grass with the other kids. That was one of the wonderful things about small town living. Paris has about

10,000 people. She pointed out to Ursey the corner store where her mother bought some of her fancier dresses for special events. The store's name had changed, but it was still there. On the other corner was the J.C. Penney store where they bought her everyday clothes. They drove north on Main Street past where she had gone to grade school until at the north end of town they came to Twin Lakes. This was the recreational area of the town with shelters for picnics, swimming, goofy golf and dancing. William reminded her that this was where the annual Whitford Reunion was held also. It had started in Oakland. William had gone with his parents back in the twenties, but it had gotten so big it was moved to this bigger park with better accommodations. "Some day I'd like to look Uncle Adren up again," William said. "He was at Mom's funeral but we didn't have much time to talk." Mollie directed him back down to the high school and then to the old neighborhood where she had grown up. The house wasn't there anymore as the commercial district had taken it over, but much to her surprise she could see a length of the old steel post fence that used to separate her house from the neighbor's. She had very few opportunities or desires to return here over the years since her parents had left for warmer regions for health purposes, and also since the war had dispersed old friends to the point that she wasn't sure whom still did live in Paris. The warm weather had helped her mother for a while, but both of her parents had died, long before their time.

Having exhausted the points of interest in Paris, William pointed the car for Charleston. It was only twenty-six miles and about all there was to see was miles of farmland still unplowed in the spring. In two months this would be green with crops as good as you'll find anywhere in the world.

This was good black dirt and that was the backbone of the community and had been for a hundred and fifty years. Industries come and go, but the land stays and these people knew how to take care of it. It is flat land but good land. Land used primarily for corn and soy beans, although some grew wheat and oats. Tall silos and big barns dotted the landscape. A few farmers had cattle in pastures and occasionally one could smell a pig farm. This is the type land that William had spent his first nine years on and he loved it.

They were at Willis' before they knew it and Lou insisted on feeding them. Eating seemed to be a favorite family pastime. Soon, with Lou's insistence that they leave the children with her, the five of them loaded into one car and started back east towards Ashmore. William sat in the front with Eddie driving and Molly, Carol and Leo sharing the rear. They were going to Canaan where Leo and William had lived with their mom first, but that was also close to where Eddie had grown up. There was no direct way to get there as the Big Embarrass River meandered all over the countryside. They had to go east to cross it, and then headed north toward Oakland, so they could turn west to find Canaan. It was only a total of twelve miles, but it seemed further. As they passed through Ashmore, Eddie pointed out where their mom's home had been and where the church sat that her father had preached in. Neither was there anymore. This community was an important part of the Whitford family. They first settled here when they came to Illinois in the late 1840's. As the trip continued the subject of Orville, their father, came up. He had not even been mentioned yesterday, but they were in Orville country now and couldn't be ignored. Eddie related that Willis had said that to his knowledge Orville was still alive and living on the old home place that he had repurchased after the depression. There really wasn't anything else new. He had never made any attempt to touch base with the McGrew family to inquire about anyone. That left a little sour taste on the tongues of some of them but it didn't last. Eddie was too busy trying to locate the country road that headed west to the river bottoms where Canaan was. Canaan was just the name of a school district. There were no public buildings or stores or even a gas station. The early settlers had just given the area a name, and it remained. Eddie finally located the road and started west. Before long they were headed downhill and the road deteriorated slowly until they crossed a bridge and started to ascend again. "There's the road to Yellowhammer," Eddie told them. "That's where Grandmother grew up with her ten brothers and sisters, including Uncle Adren, but there isn't anything there any more. Hasn't been for years. The house sat right on the turn of the river, but I think the road has grown up so much that you'd have to get a local guide to find it."

As they drove slowly along, the road continually went up and down and wound around until they were headed north again. There was no flat ground until they crested a hill to see an old church sitting on the right with a cemetery next to it. William asked Leo, "Do you remember this?" Of course he did. It was the old Oak Grove Church where they attended every week with their mother, and the graveyard where little Ursie and Orvie were buried, along with Frances, their mother. Eddie turned the car onto the church grounds and they got out and walked over to the cemetery where the Whitford name was prominently displayed again and again. It wasn't a large cemetery, but it was an old one. William led them to the rear corner where two new stones sat on the gravesites of the children and their momma. When Frances died William made sure the grave got a nice stone and the almost non-existent markings on the children's graves were replaced. On Ursie's grave, beside the name and dates was the inscription, "Beautiful Little One." On Orville's grave was his nickname, "Orvie."

As they stood over the graves Molly let out a small exclamation. "William, they spelled Ursie's name wrong. Look at it."

William said, "No dear, that's the proper spelling. I just chose to spell our Ursey differently. You see, the first Ursie, Grandmother's sister, died young. She was only eleven. My sister died young and I didn't want to chance that happening again. It's foolish I know, but that's what I wanted to do. I changed the spelling." That was explanation enough for Molly. They looked around knowing that many of these stones represented family. They also went inside the church. No one was around, so they took their time and talked about all they could remember about the place. Eddie had a lot of memories.

Just north of the church was a smaller and more obscure country road that headed west and Eddie made the turn. Almost immediately the road became a one-lane road heading downhill again. Within a half-mile they were in dense trees descending to a small bridge and then straight up hill to a right turn going back north again. It was a little eerie. Eddie stopped at the turn. "Recognize anything," he asked. Both boys were looking out the left side of the car to a spot just off the road. They had heard that Orville had torn down the old place and built a new one, but didn't realize he had moved it further back to where it was barely visible from the road. The old place had been real close to the road. At the lane entrance was a mailbox with the name Trapp on it. They just looked at it for a minute and then asked Eddie to move on. Eddie hesitated. "Give me two minutes. I want to walk back there for a minute by myself. I'm over thirty years old and I've never seen the man who fathered me. I just want to go back and take one look at this man who never cared enough to claim us. I think it will help me put him behind me." Leo and William weren't too crazy about the idea but said nothing. In less than five minutes he was back, got back in and started the car again.

Up the road about the equivalent of a city block was a trailer sitting on the left, almost on the exact spot of the old school building. Leo said, "About the only thing that I see that looks familiar is the big hump there in front. I'll bet that's the old storm shelter that's had sod put on it and is being used for something else now. Look up the road William. Does that bring back any memories?" William looked but only saw another corner with some trees and a small pond. He didn't respond so Leo went on to tell him. "There used to be a little house there with a small shed. The people had a billy goat that you thought you could ride."

Recognition now came to William's face. "Now I remember. I could have ridden him too if he hadn't of had horns. He was mean."

"He could outrun you, too," Leo said laughingly. "He butted you all the way home."

The rest of the trip through Canaan's winding roads didn't take very long. They could see the tree line where the Embarrass weaved its way and places where old houses used to stand. Most of them had not been replaced. The croplands now hid most of the old home sights. They debated stopping at the Snider's house. John still lived there with his wife. They remembered how good the elder Sniders, and then John their son, had been to Frances. John had been at Frances' funeral. "Can you imagine what those roads were like before they got graveled?" Eddie asked.

Leo and William both said, "Yes we can," at the same time.

"It took a horse to get through," Leo added.

That prompted William to tell Eddie and the women about old Mabel. "What a good old horse she was," he said. "She'd be worked all day in the field and then Mom would load us all on her back for a trip or two around the yard. We really looked forward to that. Leo got to ride her once in awhile on his own, but the rest of us were too young. Years later I would fantasize about her when I'd be watching cowboy movies with Tom Mix and Tony his horse and others, and in my mind Mabel was just as beautiful as any of them. Of course we never owned a saddle but Mabel was always very gentle and patient. I wonder what ever became of her?"

Eddie said, "I remember Gene Autry's and Roy Roger's horses better. Remember Champion and Trigger? But I know what you're saying. In my mind some of those old plow horses seemed just as good."

They made a brief tour of Oakland, a community of about a thousand people, and then headed back south on the Oakland/Ashmore road to Charleston. About half way Eddie indicated off in the distance where he and his mother had lived with the Knight family all those years ago when he was growing up. For whatever reason he didn't go past the house and his brothers sensed that he really wasn't interested in talking about those years very much. William thought it strange. In the years he had visited Frances she had always let him know how good Big Jess Knight had been to her. Although he was a hard man to know and didn't have very

49

many social graces, she had said his help saved her life more than once.

Leo took this opportunity to say, "Eddie, did you see the old man back there when we stopped?"

Eddie thought a minute and said, "Yes, he was back there sitting on his porch watching us. He didn't get up from his chair, but I could see he had a cane nearby. He seemed very old and bent over. I just asked him where the Sniders lived and he gave me directions. I told him we were just passing through. As I turned to leave he asked my name. Without looking back I said Eddie, Eddie Trapp, and kept on walking." With that there was silence as each man was deep in his own thoughts.

Back in Charleston, Eddie drove past where the Children's Home had once been. It was now a badly deteriorating old storage building with weeds growing up around it in a bad neighborhood. William answered Leo's questions about what had happened to Mr. Kirkley, the superintendent who had engineered the adoptions. They started remembering some of the names of boys they had known in the home. "Remember Carl, the little fellow with a shrunken leg?" William said. "He was in the home until he graduated from high school. Willis said he spent the war years working and scraping until he had enough to start a parts store. Today he has two or three of them."

After a short visit with Willis they said their goodbyes and pledged again their intent to stay in touch. Eddie started his nine hundred mile trip to Colorado. William was glad he only had to go to Webster Groves and Leo started north toward Rockford. Leo knew that he'd be home by midnight barring car trouble. He was anxious to see his family.

Chapter 9

❧❧

Ted's New Job

By the time the brothers had gotten to Canaan, Ted and his family were already settled back in their home in Alexandria and resting up from their trip. The kids had enjoyed the flight and wanted to talk about the big adventure they had. Joyce and Ted were content to sit and watch them and enjoy the thoughts of the two days they had just spent in Indiana. Ted was more than satisfied with the way things had gone and for a few hours he'd been able to forget the pressures he'd been experiencing on the job the last few weeks. He had been reassigned the first of January at the Pentagon and was struggling with his job assignment.

The following Monday morning Ted was at his desk reviewing a stack of folders clearly marked Top Secret. He was a full colonel assigned by the Army Chief of Staff as the military liaison to the Secretary of the Army. As such, he worked closely with one of the under-secretaries in his field of expertise, which was troop training and deployment. Since graduating from the Point in 1950, he had never held a command over an army group, but had served in administrative capacities for over eleven years at various levels. After the war, where he had served as a lieutenant in a combat company, Ted was never really interested in that type of command again. His talents, and the fact that he graduated with honors from the academy, had helped him move through the ranks more quickly than most of his peers. Ted didn't kid himself though, because he knew his family connections and war record were instrumental in propelling his career, but he was not apologetic for it. He was a good administrator and he liked what he was doing. At least he had up until now.

On January 1st he stepped into an ongoing operation named Puma that he was having trouble fully understanding. It was a Top Secret project and his job was to coordinate secret efforts to train and stage army personnel. He had to satisfy both the army and civilian leadership. Because there were many considerations involved and branches of government not normally connected to such a project, Ted was seeing a lot of indecision at the top echelon of command and government. The CIA had operatives that wanted control because of the Cuban exiles involved. The Air Force, to some extent, thought they should have more control because of their critical involvement. In truth, the only real control was the civilian control at the top, the president. Communications were terrible because they were on a need-to-know basis. People trying to coordinate the operation, and Ted was one such person, did not even know their counterparts in the other branches of the military and government.

He didn't feel good about the impending action that planners had started devising under the Eisenhower administration. It was now continuing under the new president who had been on the job even less time than he had.

Zero hour had been set for April 10th and Ted was still trying to get assurances back from army military commanders that the special training was being accomplished. He needed to know that the logistical plans were being carried out without the lid of secrecy being blown off. Someone was calling the shots, but Ted couldn't believe that it was the new president with all of his other responsibilities.

He had just returned from a top-level meeting a few days later when his secretary buzzed him and said he had a visitor. In walked Joe Brown, his old roommate from West Point. As he and Joe pumped each other's hand, Ted was reminded how much of a physical specimen and mental giant this man was. Joe spoke. "I'm here for a few days and will be working just down the hall. My first priority is seeing you." As they exchanged pleasantries, Ted had his secretary cancel his other luncheon engagement and had her call his wife to see if it would be all right to bring Joe and his wife home for dinner this evening. She rang back and said that was a go. Ted and Joe proceeded to lunch where they caught up on each other's activities. Joe had taken a different route since graduation. He had seen combat in Korea, served a three year tour in Japan, and had just returned from a short tour in Hawaii. He had always been a line commander and as such had done very well, having just received his eagles as a colonel. He was now stationed at Fort Benning, Georgia, as second in command of a regiment. He couldn't have been happier with his progress.

"What papers are you shuffling my young colonel?" Joe asked.

"Nothing I can tell you about, my friend," Ted replied. They brought each other up to date on other classmates and friends. In Ted's mind, he knew the prediction he had made years ago regarding Joe would one day come true. This man was going to be a General of the Army and Chief of Staff some day. They both were still young, thirty-seven and thirty-eight respectively, but the real leader of men was, without a doubt, Joe.

Later that evening, as they were having cocktails before dinner, Ted couldn't help but note that while Donna was as pretty as ever, there was a change, and he thought it was mainly reflected in her eyes. Other than that, she was just an older version of the little belle he had met in 1946 and wooed for over four years, only to lose her to his best buddy Joe. It had been three years since he had seen her and they had a lot of catching up to do. Joyce and Donna had met at Donna and Joe's wedding in 1952 and had corresponded ever since. Ted was a little surprised that they hadn't started a family by now and said so. "Joe, you should try this family thing, it grows on you."

Joe responded. "I think we're about where we need to be now to consider that. I'm done with foreign deployment for a while and Donna can finally get settled into a nice place for a change. Maybe it'll happen."

Donna didn't comment on that but said, "Is anyone having seconds. I can use one." Ted hurriedly got her and Joe another drink. The children joined them at the table and little Ursey was the hit of the ball. Both Donna and Joe couldn't get over her.

The women cleared the dishes after dinner and Joe and Ted retired to the den. Joe wasn't quite his usual self and Ted asked him if everything was okay. He'd lived with the man for four years and been his best man, so he thought he could at least ask the question. He was right. Joe did seem to want to talk about his marriage. "You know how Donna used to tell you when you were dating that she didn't want a military life?" Joe asked. "Well she still hasn't changed her mind. She would like nothing better than for me to resign my commission and find another job. She's even suggested that I apply for your father's position at VMI. Her family told her of his pending resignation and she's serious about it. She misses her society things. We've never been in one place long enough for her to get into the inner circle of the in-group, and you know how she always thrived on that type of thing. She's just not happy and I don't think there will be a family until she is." Joe paused to let that soak in.

Ted responded, "I know that she never would change for me, but I thought that when she married you she might have come around. I'm beginning to think that maybe she can't change."

Joe mumbled, "I don't think I can either. I'm not ready for an academic position at age thirty-eight. I need more of a challenge than that."

At the end of the evening they agreed upon taking in a play and dinner the following week before the Browns returned to Georgia. Donna said she'd be driving down to VMI for a couple of days to visit her parents but would be back for the dinner. Ted walked them both out to the car and opened the door for Donna while Joe went around to the other side. Donna whispered, "I'll call you."

He returned to the house wondering what that was all about and mentioned it to Joyce. "Some things are bothering that girl," Joyce said. "You were his close friend for years and maybe you can help." Ted told Joyce about Joe's conversation then and wished the evening had ended on a higher note. They had so much and appeared to enjoy it so little.

Chapter 10

ॐॐ

Home In Rockford

The trip from Charleston to Rockford is not an exciting trip. Carol and Leo were on two-lane highways most of the way, but fortunately the weather was good and the traffic light. The trip gave them an excellent chance to hash and rehash all they had experienced the last forty-eight hours. Leo shared all he had learned from his conversations with the brothers and Carol told all she knew. This made the time pass quickly. It also gave them the time to rehearse all they would tell their children, who were about to find out that they had a number of relatives they had never met. Carol only had one brother and they weren't close, and that was the extent of the family up to now. They were about to gain another six cousins, several aunts and uncles and even some great aunts and uncles. They sensed their children would take the news quite well, but they still wanted to pass the information along without totally overwhelming them. How much could a twelve-year-old boy and an eight-year-old girl absorb in a short period of time. Carol said, "We're not pressed for time. They can get the details over a period of time. I'm glad we have pictures to develop to show them." Carol had wanted more children after Katie was born but it hadn't happened. Now at forty she was very happy with the two she had.

The lights were still on in the living room when they pulled into the drive of their home. They knew the parents were still up. They let themselves in the backdoor and through the kitchen where fresh coffee was on the stove and a freshly baked pie on the sideboard. The kids would have been in bed for over an hour and should be asleep, but that was not a major concern as tomorrow was not a school day. Leo's mother met them at the kitchen door and gave them both a hug. His father roused himself from a nap, although he would have denied that he was asleep. They told the parents that the trip had been just great and they had much to share. However, they were worn out and decided that sharing over breakfast when they were fresh would probably be best for all concerned. They also wanted them there when the kids were told. Leo did have time for pie and coffee before he turned in though, and his dad joined him. They said their goodnights and headed upstairs. The kids had shared a bedroom so that the grandparents could have William's room that night.

Katie woke them the next morning by jumping in bed with them. She was rested and eager to talk to them. She couldn't remember ever being separated from them for three days. "Grandma almost has breakfast ready," she said. "She's doing blueberry pancakes. Hurry and get up." It was a happy breakfast atmosphere with the children bouncing around, full of energy, bombarding them with questions about their trip. They avoided most of their questions until after they had eaten. They then suggested they all go to the living room where they could be more comfortable. The men sat in the chairs and the women snuggled up with the children on the sofa.

Leo started. "The trip to Terre Haute your mother and I took turned out to be something very special. We're sorry now that we didn't take you with us, but we weren't sure what was going to be happening. This isn't an easy story to tell and you're going to have lots of questions. They may not all get answered today, but we want to at least give you the basic story. This can be a sad story, but because we can talk about it today makes it a happy story. We've been blessed with a wonderful family and you two are the most important part of it.

"Your grandparents and I had a very special beginning. I came to them as a young boy without a home and needing a lot of special love and care to get me through a sad and scary part of my life."

William said softly, "You mean you weren't born their baby?"

"That's true son," Leo said, "I was born to a woman who had several children. Due to no fault of her own she couldn't take care of us and had to give us up for adoption for others to raise." Katie's eyes got big, as she looked first at her daddy and then her mother.

"Just listen to your daddy and I think you'll be happy for him in what he has to tell," Carol said.

Leo continued. "I was eleven years old and was living in a Children's Home down in Southern Illinois. The Children's Home is where they take care of children with special needs or ones that don't have parents that can take care of them or are orphans. In addition to me there were three brothers. We were placed there when our mother couldn't take care of us.

Later she got very ill and everyone thought she was dying. We didn't have a daddy. He had already left home and the people in charge decided that it would be best if they could find us another home rather than let us grow up there without a mother or a father. There were about twenty other children in the home and from time to time some were adopted, but some had to stay there until they were old enough to go to work. Most of the time the people looking for children could only adopt one, and that's why my brothers and I were separated. That's the only way they could find us all homes. It was in the difficult depression years and people couldn't afford to feed four more mouths. The home they found for me was Grandma and Granddad's. They wanted to be here today because they want you to know the story now that you're old enough to understand. We think telling you the story now will add to your lives and only make us a happier family."

Carol could tell by the emotion in Leo's voice that he needed a little break so she spoke up. "These last two days we have been with most of your daddy's brothers that he was separated from when he was a boy. It was only recently that he found where they were and they decided they wanted to get to know each other all over. Other parents had adopted each of them and now they are happy men like you father, but they also want to know us and you and our whole family. We didn't tell you about this before we went because we didn't want to disappoint you if it didn't all turn out okay. We're telling you because we found some wonderful people. I know this is all overwhelming and you have lots of questions, but Daddy has three living brothers with wives and kids, aunts and uncles. The youngest of their six children is two and the oldest ten. In a couple of days we'll have the pictures we took developed and you'll see some of them. Two of the children couldn't come this time, but their daddy promised to send us pictures."

Grandma Swenson then spoke up. "We are so happy for your daddy and for you. We often wished we could have given your daddy brothers and sisters but we couldn't. All of our family was left behind in the old country so your daddy never had much family growing up. For a long time he was a scared, sad, and lonely little boy and only became truly happy when he found your momma and you children were born. And now to have found more family just adds to his happiness and will to yours too. You're granddad and I think its just wonderful."

Leo wept as he listened to this and when she finished turned to his children. "This is so much at one time, but do you have any questions for us before we go on."

William spoke up. "Where do these people live and will we get to see them?"

"You sure will," his dad replied. "In fact we plan to meet at least once a year and maybe more. They live pretty far away but we'll manage it. Eddie, my youngest brother lives in Colorado with his wife and two kids. The next youngest is Ted and he lives near Washington, D.C., in Virginia. They have two children also, a boy and a girl. My brother just two years younger than me is a minister and he also lives in Virginia. Guess what? His name is William. I named you after him when you were born son. I've never forgotten him. He has a wife and two children also. We have pictures of them."

Katie spoke up. "Who was I named after?"

Her mother said, "We just thought Kathleen was a beautiful name."

Their questions were what kids want to know about other kids and they laughed and joked while sharing a lot of little trivia about family. Carol knew that sooner or later they would get around to asking about Leo's birth mother and father, but there was no reason to talk about it until they were ready.

All at once Katie bounced up off the sofa and jumped into her daddy's lap. She wrapped her arms around his neck and said, "I'm so happy for you daddy. You found your brothers." That was Leo's little cheerleader. Just like her mother, he thought. Then she surprised him. "Daddy, am I adopted?"

He hugged her long and hard and said, "No darling, we have to claim both you and your brother. You grew right there in Mommy's stomach."

Carol sent the kids off to get dressed for the day. She and Leo sat talking with his folks sharing as much as they could remember about the encounter. They had read William's letter that Leo had shared with them months earlier and now Leo was just filling in the cracks. Bottom line, they looked forward to the day when they might have the chance to meet some of these people. Leo need never to have worried how they would take the information of him wanting to hook up with his past. They were wonderful.

Leo shared the news with his fellow workers also. They were surprised but happy for him. He had been with the Rockford branch of motor vehicles for over six years and had a good group to work with. His job as license inspector for the state had come around in a strange way. While they normally came as a result of political involvement, the last few months had shed significant light on how he'd really gotten the job. He found out that his birth mother's uncle was the personnel manager for the Secretary of the State and had spotted his application and recognized who he was and pulled a few strings. What a small world it was and his fellow employees were interested in his story. Some of them revealed that they had used a little clout themselves to get their jobs. Of course, at the time Leo didn't know he had any clout. Politics changed from time to time in the state but Leo felt pretty secure now. He had stayed as non-political as possible, but was still a registered Republican. He just did his job, abided by the rules, and trusted that his professionalism, education, and good war record would be enough. At forty-three he wasn't looking to make a mid-life occupation change. The benefits were good and Rockford was a good community to raise his family in. His friends noted that he seemed to have a new spring in his step and was a happier man than they had noted before the new revelations. Leo was thinking that maybe one day soon he'd call that cousin who had contacted him last year about his birth mother. He hadn't been very nice at that time and thought maybe a dinner out with he and his wife might be a nice thing to do. He made a mental note to call them.

Chapter 11

❧❧

The Bay of Pigs

There was a message on his desk that Colonel Brown had called and regretfully cancelled their dinner engagement. He'd been recalled to his post and Ted thought it probably had to do with the Puma project he was working on. It was April 12 and all systems were go for Operation Puma, and although he and Joe had never discussed it, Ted was not surprised that Joe was involved in some way. Because of the need-to-know secrecy, Ted didn't even know how things were to be initiated. Surely the White House was not going to give the go ahead on invading Cuba without some provocation. Hopefully the intelligence agencies were on top of things. All he knew was that a battalion of soldiers had been trained for an amphibious assault and deployed to a secret location. Backing that group up was a regiment on standby at Ft. Benning. He assumed the other services had similar preparations. The Army had supplied equipment for a Cuban exile group at a secret base in conjunction with the CIA, but Ted did not have a very good feeling of the way that was handled. In fact, Ted was uneasy about what was due to commence in less than seventy-two hours. He certainly had no love for Castro, but the U.S. history was you don't provoke, but respond. We'd been provoked at Pearl Harbor. We were drawn in by enemy action against our shipping in the European war, and we had rallied to support an ally in Korea, but this plan sounded different. Within months of an administrative change, the U.S. was preparing for what appeared to be a planned invasion. This was serious.

Joyce was disappointed when Ted had to cancel out on the theatre and suggested that she take a friend. He had been under tremendous pressure lately and although he couldn't talk about it, she was sure that something major was happening or due to transpire soon. He had not been happy in this new assignment and she hoped things would change soon. As she watched the evening news there wasn't a hint of any military action in the world except a small story on Indochina, and that seemed like a remote possibility. She just had to be supportive, understanding, and patient and pray this would all blow over soon. She was raised as an army brat and had seen it happen with her own parents.

On the morning of April 15, 1961, three flights of aircraft bombed and strafed the airfields of Cuba as a counter-offensive against the Cuban Revolutionary Forces. Two days later, four chartered transports carrying fifteen hundred Cuban exiles were landed on Cuban soil at the Bay of Pigs on the southern coast. Supporting them were two landing craft, under the command of the CIA, containing supplies and equipment. The plan was for the exiles to join up with rebels opposing Castro's government and to move quickly to control the island. Supposedly the air power of the Cuban forces had been destroyed. Ted was in the war room at the

Pentagon with his staff on standby for any emergency that might arise where he might be called on. He only returned home to change clothes and take short rests and say hello to the children. The first morning there had been a summit meeting of the Joint Chiefs of Staff, that he was not invited to, and the under-secretary of the army was communicating directly with them instead of through him, the liaison officer. He was left in the dark except to note the progress, or lack of progress, on the maps in the war room. Unknown to him, the Air Force plan to send multiple missions from a base in Nicaragua had been changed and the initial air attack was the only one made. The reason that the invasion was delayed two days was unclear and there were no answers forthcoming. Even before the landing took place on the 17th there was much consternation and many of the key general officers were not in the war room. The news turned badly very quickly after the invasion started and word was the rebel army had not or could not hook up with the invading exile troops and there was a lot of confusion and opposition to the landing. Things were in a state of chaos and there was nothing Ted could do but watch. The intelligence reported that somehow Castro had found and executed key rebel commanders even before the invasion began, and several hundred thousand Cubans had been imprisoned, making the rebel army only a shell of what it was supposed to be. The order was never given to reinforce the exiles with the troops held in reserve, nor were additional supplies moved in. By the 19th the battle was over and it was a victory for the Republic of Cuba. The pall around the Pentagon was unbelievable and high-ranking officers of all services could not even look one another in the eye. What had happened? Could this have happened to the strongest military in the world? On the nineteenth Ted was told by the under-secretary to convey the message that all manpower and materials on secret deployment should immediately be returned to their home bases. He and his staff went to work immediately to get these orders circulated and within twenty-four hours it was done. He dragged himself home where he hoped he could sleep for a week and this nightmare would disappear. Someone would have to pay dearly for this fiasco and Ted was literally ill. What a waste. What a sacrifice of men. The news media was just beginning to carry details to the American people that would be hard to explain. The world press was already hearing from Castro and getting his version of the battle.

Chapter 12

࿔

The Aftermath

William couldn't believe what he was seeing on the evening news and he called Ted to learn what it was all about. It was the 16th and Joyce said that Ted had only been home for a few hours over the past few days to change clothes and catch a nap. He was spending almost all of his time at the office. She would let him know that William had called. William told her to let them know if he and Molly could be of any help.

They had stayed in Webster Groves with his parents until the last week of March. The Watsons had been delighted at the report of how the reunion had gone and had enjoyed all the pictures Molly had taken. Aunt Marilyn and her husband, who lived in Springfield, Illinois, visited while they were there, so the Watsons just had a reunion, too. Ursey had missed a little school, but she was very sharp and would easily catch up. William enjoyed seeing his mother and her sister together. Normally, his mother was a quiet person, but when Aunt Marilyn was around it was a non-stop gabfest. No topic was too big or too small. They went on for hours, usually interrupting each other and finishing each other's sentences without ever losing a beat. The men went into another room when they wanted to talk.

While there, William explored some things that could result in him making a change in his ministry. Academically he was fulfilled, having received his Doctorate of Divinity, and the last ten years in Falls Church were certainly rewarding, but he was seeing things in the greater St. Louis area that started him thinking of other things he could or possibly should be doing. He and Molly discussed it. They decided to pray on it for a while to see if it was God's will. It would bring him back home, for one thing, at a time when his parents were getting to be most vulnerable. The Midwest was Molly's home also, but that wasn't the thing that meant the most. The national office had offered him other churches at different times, but that wasn't what he felt called to do. He just wanted to serve where he could fill the biggest need, and as he looked around sections of St. Louis he saw a big need. Webster Groves was not a mission field, but it was within miles of plenty of areas needing real outreach. God had provided that he never needed for financial security, so he could well afford to go where the need existed and where maybe the ability to pay a minister did not. He talked to the area ministerial alliance and was encouraged and directed to places where spiritual needs were not being met, but also where people were desperate for housing and food. Molly supported his thinking totally. She felt she could best contribute by putting her medical training to use. They would go back home and talk it over with Ted. They had grown so close, and that was the one drawback. They didn't like the idea of being separated from him and his family again.

Ted had not returned his call a few days later and William was thinking of this as he unfolded the morning paper. There in banner headlines were the words, "Heads to Roll for Cuban Fiasco." As he read the articles he was further depressed by their content. If this was true, what could the U.S. government have been thinking? One story said that Castro claimed he had prior knowledge of the impending invasion and acted accordingly in controlling the interior opposition. He said he had eyes and ears in the American government. Another article said that the foreign press was reporting from reliable sources that the U.S. military had staged friendly fire on their own aircraft as justification to respond against the Cuban government. Editorials were asking why an invasion, once undertaken, was allowed to fail. Much was being made of the Cuban exiles being left to die on the beaches, murdered by Soviet guns and tanks while there were staged manpower and equipment never used to reinforce them. One article asked, "Were Cuban lives so cheap?" William was especially distraught that Ted might have gotten caught up in all of this. Did the president authorize this action, or was this a military foul-up? He paused to pray for his brother and for the leadership of the nation, as well as those destroyed at the Bay of Pigs.

Ted was driving to the Pentagon with similar thoughts on his mind. Over the course of these four days it was evident that the early change in the plans on the invasion made the overall battle plan untenable. So much relied on the Cuban rebels being able to hook up with the landing forces, and then the targeted area was moved out of their reach. Who had made that decision? Who was the architect that all but guaranteed the failure? All of his misgivings had come true. An ill-conceived idea, tragically executed, had brought world condemnation on the U.S. and its military. Who would pay?

At the office he returned his brother's call and planned for the families to get together for dinner the next evening. William said he would pray for him and Ted knew he would need that strength in the days ahead. He thought about what he had been lacking in his life. Although he and Joyce attended worship service regularly, he was not as connected as he should have been. He had been raised to be self-sufficient and he was learning now that wasn't enough. He needed more. He was happy that William was in his life. He could talk it out with him. He was very comfortable talking to his brother about anything.

The top brass were not visible again this morning as he walked the hallways of the Pentagon. In his office he had a call waiting from Joe at Fort Benning wanting to know what was going on. Ted couldn't satisfy his inquiry, as he was definitely not in the circle of need-to-know. Joe told him. "Watch yourself friend, watch your back, they'll have someone for this." Ted knew he was right. The military brass were already being called to Congressional hearings, although no one was admitting that this was any thing but an exile uprising at this point.

A week later Ted was summoned to the office of personnel and met with the executive officer there. He was advised that he was being reassigned and his orders would be drawn at the end of the month letting him know where he would be going. He was to turn his records over to his assistant and bring him up to date in the interim. Ted immediately asked for the committee review that he was entitled to. He was advised that he had every right to do so, but that a letter had already been placed in his file, by the Chief of Staff, reprimanding him for his action in the ill-fated Puma Project. Ted saw the handwriting on the wall. That one letter was the death sentence for a career officer hoping to hold a general's rank. He walked out of that office with only one thing on his mind. He wanted to consult with his father. He knew he was not the only one getting summoned that week, but he knew he was not deserving of this treatment. The media had to have their scapegoats and the brass had found a way to place the blame. Ted doubted that any general officers would be included.

He and Joyce had a long discussion that night. It was hard to believe that this could happen but he was sure it wasn't all that rare in the military. It would be over three years before he was eligible for early retirement and his superiors were counting on him taking his lumps and staying the course for that long. Other officers who had their time in might choose to go public and fight the injustice. That would be an embarrassment to the military and possibly cause the blame to seek a higher level. Despite the injustice, Ted was not inclined to create a scandal for all of the good men in uniform because of just a few. And besides, he wasn't all that sure it was just the military. He would go see his father to seek his guidance, but he was also long overdue for a visit to see his mother, who had been quite ill. His job had kept him here when he should have been with her.

As he drove along alone, he was thinking about the dinner he had with William a few nights ago. Joyce had stayed behind so Ursey wouldn't have to miss more school. The meeting with William had helped so much. His brother, by listening, had helped him see for himself that it would not have been humanly possible to change the chain of events these past weeks. People with much more authority were given the responsibility of oversight and they had dropped the ball.

Congress has sitting committees for that purpose and the ability to make a difference. The timing was crucial. With the change of Congress and the change of the presidency right at a critical time in the planning, the ball had indeed been dropped. Now it was up to Ted to do what was best for his family. At the end of the evening he had asked William and the wives to join him in prayer. Ted led the prayer as they stood holding hands. He didn't pray for his job to be saved. He didn't ask for God to show others his innocence. Instead, he prayed for his country and its leadership at all levels. He prayed for God to be with his family and he confessed out loud that he had indeed been haughty and self-sufficient and now wished to put his life in God's hands. "Help me be a better father and husband," he had prayed. For the first time in his life he could see clearly that someone was there for him, and that he wanted to acknowledge it now and forever. Amidst all the turmoil of this time, he knew he was blessed. He and William had shed happy tears that night together.

When he arrived at the commandant's mansion he found his mother bed-ridden and his father at her side. Ted was shocked at her frail appearance. After sitting with them for a while, he told his parents of his trip to Indiana and the reunion of the brothers. He didn't talk about his job, and because they didn't ask, he assumed they were not into the news picture at this time. He'd fill his dad in later. He told them all about Molly and William, who they had come to love, and the children. He had pictures.

The Wainright family had never been a spiritual family. They attended church and did all the right things, but worship was a Sunday affair and one didn't talk about one's religion. They didn't fully understand the change they were seeing in their son, but they liked the man they were seeing. They had seen much the same thing in William. He had been a good influence. Even so, it was strange to them when Ted wanted to pray with them. He felt moved to pray for his parents, especially his mother. After the prayer his mother thanked him for his loving concern. She was tiring, so Ted and his father went downstairs so she could get some rest. Her eyes were closed before they got out the door.

Ted didn't want to burden his father further by dwelling on the wrongs that had been perpetrated against him. Instead, he merely told him of his reassignment and that there was a lot happening in the aftermath of the Bay of Pigs fiasco. Being a retired general, his father didn't need an explanation. The military had not changed that much from the years that he was actively involved. While he was angry with them for his son's treatment, he would defer to his son's judgment as to how he wanted to handle it. He would support him in any way he could. They talked for some time, mostly about his mother, and his father returned to her side where the maid would be bringing their dinner. Ted excused himself and said he'd eat later. For now he'd take a walk.

The campus in the early evening light was still beautiful despite the fact that there were no flowers blooming yet. Ted enjoyed observing the activity of the cadets and decided to sit on one of the stone benches to watch the sun set. He was sitting there thinking of his mother's health when he heard his name called. He turned and there was Donna striding toward him. He was surprised to see her and told her so. "I heard the commandant's son was on campus and came to see for myself," she said. "How is your mother today? Mother has been keeping me up to date on her condition. I hope she's resting comfortably." Ted said she was.

"I'm surprised to see you here Donna. I thought you and Joe would be back at Benning."

"Oh, he is," Donna said. "He is very busy and didn't need me around to distract him the past couple of weeks. I'm surprised you could get away with all the hub-bub."

Ted filled her in on his reasons without going into any great detail. Donna sat down on the bench and they made small talk for a while until the evening chill prompted Ted to say he'd better be getting back. It was then that Donna got serious.

"Ted, I need your help. I told you I'd call you, but that didn't work out. We go way back and I know you can tell I'm not happy. I'm not made to be an army wife, and being one is just making me resent Joe more and more as the years go by. I don't think our marriage is going to survive. Why can't he be more like you? You're a husband first and then military. He has his priorities backward and won't change. Can't you help me convince him?" With that she removed a small flask from her purse, and making sure there were no cadets in the vicinity she raised it to her lips. She offered it to Ted, but he just nodded no.

"Donna, I think your husband realizes the seriousness of the situation and wants to make it work, but are you truly doing all you can? I'll talk to him and encourage him to get his priorities in order, but I think you need to do that also. What is your priority? If it's not your marriage, then I think it had better be. Can't the two of you find some deeper meaning to your lives than ambition for a career or popularity in society? Do either of you still go to church or read your Bible?"

With that comment, Donna just stared at Ted. This wasn't what she had expected from him. This man had loved

76

her at one time and she knew it. Why was he talking like a counselor or a minister? She wanted comfort from him, not lectures. She didn't need to hear this from him. In her state of mind, she couldn't handle that and quickly got up and walked away. "You call me if you really want to help me," she called back over her shoulder.

Ted just sat there awhile before returning to the mansion. He couldn't help but reflect on the timing of all this. What would have happened a year ago, or even a month ago? He would have faced a temptation that he might not have handled properly. He prayed he'd be strong enough this time. At bedtime that night Ted started a new practice. Before sleep he had an extended prayer time.

The next morning he said his goodbyes, but not before his parents had explained their plans. They had good friends in a retirement community in Tucson who had located a spot for them and they were moving there the first of July. They regretted moving so far away from Ted and his family but thought it best at this time. Ted wasn't too sure where he would be by the end of the summer himself and said so. He explained that wherever they were, he'd come as often as possible to see them. They explained that the board of regents were throwing a special retirement party for them and they hoped Ted and Joyce would be able to make it. It was scheduled for the fourth week of June. Ted assured them he'd be back and that William and Molly would probably want to come also.

Chapter 13

๛

Eddie's Business Woes

It had been six months since Eddie's trip to Terre Haute. Eddie was sweeping and mopping after a long day. He had closed for the evening and was thinking about his latest phone call from William. He was happy to hear that circumstances might be bringing him back to the Midwest. This might be a way that they could see each other more often and grow closer. He was anxious for Barb to get to know his entire family better. As he mopped, he couldn't help but reflect on his wife and kids. What would he do without them? He wanted much more for them, but for now they were struggling and doing without a lot. He wanted his children to have the real security that he never had. It had been a lucky day when Barb's brothers had coaxed him to come home with them one weekend. They had worked together for several months and really hit it off well. They were wild and crazy guys, but good guys. One Saturday after work he took them up on their invitation and came to Cheyenne Wells for dinner at their home. "One more plate won't mean anything to my mom," Alphonse had said. When Eddie walked in the door with them he began to wonder. There seemed to be kids everywhere, but it turned out fine. It got to be a Saturday night habit and Eddie began to feel he was a part of something. This large family absorbed him like a sponge and it wasn't six months before one of the girls became very special to him. The girls were in the minority in the household, but Barb became the most important one to Eddie. She had a zest for life and an enthusiasm that Eddie couldn't resist. She could also be loud and tomboyish, but each time Eddie saw her his feelings grew stronger, and apparently it was mutual. The first time he asked her out she said, "What took you so long?" Surprisingly, he didn't get much interference from her older brothers, even though she was still in high school. They only made one comment about it, that they'd kill him if he mistreated her. Their relationship turned out to be the real deal and they were married with everyone's blessing.

Eddie had always prayed and he knew his Bible. His mom had made sure of that. In his travels, though, he didn't even own one. He had never known any family life except that with the Knight family where his mother had worked all those years. His mom had nurtured him and loved him everyday of his life, but there was something missing. The security of that place could be lost in a heartbeat and he knew it. Furthermore, one of the Knight boys made sure he didn't forget it. As difficult as times were now, trying to make a living, he knew he had a real family among her kin that were there for them.

Big Jess, or Mr. Knight as Eddie's mom always made sure he called him, always treated Eddie okay. He was distant and unapproachable to him and even to his own boys. Eddie was too young to understand, but understood later when he realized he was only the hired help's kid. Jim, Big Jess' oldest son, looked after Eddie when he was around, but he wasn't always there. When Eddie started to school he became just another kid to the two younger boys. Burdette, the older one of the two, started punching him around a lot. He was three years older and loved to inflict pain on both him and Danny. He didn't do it when Jim was around because Jim would give him some of the same, but it got pretty bad sometimes when Jim wasn't around. It got so Danny would punch him sometimes too just to imitate his older brother, but he didn't do it for the joy of it. He was just following an example set for him. Normally it would happen away from the house where Eddie's mom couldn't hear. At first it was just punches in the arm, but then he found he could hurt more by punching Eddie in the stomach and back. Eddie told his mother a couple of times and she would scold Burdette and tell him to stop. Finally she confronted Burdette in front of his father. Mr. Knight didn't do much more than lift an eyebrow, but did say, "You boys quit picking on boys smaller than yourselves. If you want to fight, find someone your own age. Frances, boys are going to be boys." The next time Burdette got him alone he punched him hard in the stomach, enough to make him fall to his knees. "You know what will happen if you ever squeal on me again, don't you? My dad will kick you and your mom out and you'll probably die without a home." Eddie believed him. He was about seven, and he never ran to Momma again. Even when Burdette busted his nose, he didn't tell. They were actually playing that time, running in the barn and chasing one another. He came around one of the stalls at a run and slipped and fell just as Burdette was swinging the wooden end of a pitchfork at his knees. It caught him across the bridge of the nose instead, smashing it.

Burdette was immediately sorry but threatened him anyhow. "It was an accident so just say you fell or something and hit your head," he told Eddie. He threatened Danny, too. They helped him to the house where his mom cleaned him up and examined the badly bent cartilage. Mr. Knight took his nose and pinched it together and said he thought it would be okay. "We'll just keep it taped a few days and it'll heal," he said. After the initial pain, it wasn't that bad unless he hit it or turned the wrong way in his sleep. After that, Burdette didn't pick on him as much. When he was about fourteen or fifteen he found better things to do. Eddie could just about imagine the type of man he'd become. After high school he didn't wait around to see. He knew it broke his mom's heart when he left home as soon as he could, but he had to find a life. If that was family life, he definitely wanted to try something different. Since leaving home he had only seen Jim and Dan one time, and that was at his mom's funeral. Burdette had not come.

Barb's family was different. They competed fairly, they laughed a lot, they cried at times, and they were strong people. They were also strong willed, as he was to find out. They wanted Barb to finish high school before getting married, but she and Eddie were head over heels in love and she dug her heels in. The parents were concerned about the religion thing also. They were Roman Catholic, so was half the town, and Eddie had grown up in his little Oak Grove Separatist Baptist Church and didn't even know a Catholic when he was growing up. Oakland, where he went to high school, didn't even have a Catholic Church. From what he picked up about Catholics on the street and from misinformed Sunday school teachers, they worshipped a Pope instead of Jesus. Barb set him straight on that account pretty quickly. She believed in

Jesus and went to Mass every week and worshipped Him. That was something Eddie didn't do very often. He'd go once in awhile if he had someone to go with. As much as Barb wanted to marry him, though, she wanted to be married by a priest. If Eddie wasn't willing to become a Catholic, he had to at least agree that their children would be raised Catholic. Eddie agreed to that and the priest married them. On the first trip back east with Barb to meet his mom, Eddie felt his mom had fallen in love with her immediately. His mom looked at the person and not at the religion. He had fully shared his story about Burdette with Barb, but she was the only one he ever had told. She knew it was Eddie's demon and prayed that one day he could put it behind him. After being with his brothers and experiencing them, he hoped he could. Maybe the next time he could be more open with them, and thought that would help.

As he locked up and started his walk home, his worries about the business resurfaced. It was a struggle and they were barely making it. Theirs was the only full-service restaurant in Cheyenne Wells, but there were two other bars. He didn't like the bar business, but knew if he shut it down the pool hall would go south, too, and he'd be bankrupt. He loved the restaurant business and only wished it would stand on its own, but this was a community of only a thousand people. They were in a crisis and Eddie needed to find a second job if they were going to survive financially. He'd pretty well exhausted the possibilities in town and the surrounding ranches, which meant he would need to go to the next town some twenty-five miles away. Barb knew the situation and was looking also, even though Eddie emphasized that she was already separated from the kids too much. There were more tough times ahead. They might have to pack up, let the bank have the business, and move to Denver where he could find employment. The house was dark as he approached and he knew everyone had turned in for the night. He looked up the block and saw lights on at the in-laws', but he was too tired to make the trip. He wasn't very good company that night anyway.

Chapter 14

❧ ❧

The Inheritance

Leo already had plans for the next get together with his brothers. He was excited that some of them had moved closer and hoped this would make for more visiting over the years. He had talked to William again over the Christmas holidays, and they'd decided to see if everyone could arrange to meet around Memorial Day. The location was up in the air, but Kansas City was a possibility. The kids would be out of school and the weather would not be a problem. Leo felt it would be a perfect vacation time for his family. They'd never been west of Des Moines and this might be the perfect time and year to show the kids the Rocky Mountains. William had called back and confirmed the Memorial Day date and said Kansas City was acceptable to all. Things had gone so well in Terre Haute; he wanted his children to get to know their cousins, aunts, and uncles. Katie asked him about them all the time. On several occasions the children had pinned him down, wanting to know more about those early years.

He found he could talk more easily all the time about the good memories. He enjoyed reliving those early days.

Leo was thinking about this when the phone rang. Carol was out for the evening and the kids were in bed so he got up to answer. "Is this Leo Swenson?" the voice asked. Leo said it was. "My name is Raymond Trapp, the brother of Orville Trapp." The hair stood up on Leo's neck. Wasn't it just two years ago that this type of thing had happened?

"Yes, I've heard of you," Leo said. "My mom always spoke well of you. What can I do for you?"

Raymond continued. "I got your name from your Uncle Willis and he thought it best that I contact you direct as the oldest of the surviving sons of Orville. I am well aware of the estrangement that exists between the family and Orville, but it's my responsibility to inform you of his death. His second wife, Hazel, has predeceased him, and the court has appointed me as the administrator of his estate. By law, his estate belongs to his next of kin, which are his sons. He and Hazel didn't have children, therefore you and your brothers are the sole heirs." There was a pause, as Leo didn't know what to say. He had mixed feelings about being an heir of the man that he had developed contempt for over the years, but knew he had to find out for the rest of them what this call was all about.

"Do my brothers and I have any responsibilities in regard to this matter?" he asked.

"No, the courts have given me the authority to act and the estate has no significant claims against it so far. There appears to be assets to cover all potential claims. You four are to be the only recipients of the distribution of assets after court costs. It could be significant. I do not anticipate that it will be a taxable estate under the tax law, but I will file all necessary papers and pay all fees from the proceeds. What I would like to do is find out what your wishes are regarding the real estate. I could just sell it and distribute the income, or if you so desire, meaning you and your brothers, the land could be deeded over to you. I'd like to send you a copy of the estate inventory showing you what is in it, and have you and your brothers advise me if you have any preferences regarding any of the assets before I proceed to liquidate or file legal deeds. Orville died the first of February and I'm hoping I can settle the estate and make my final report to the courts by September."

Leo said, "I will get with the others and give you our feedback as quickly as possible. I thank you for your consideration. I remember you a little from the old days and Mom told some of the other brothers how you had helped in many ways. I'd like to thank you in all our behalf. Let me have your number and I'll call you." After he hung up he could only think, "What is going to happen next?"

He didn't waste any time, as he immediately called William and told him about the unexpected contact. William said, "I don't really want anything from this man. I don't need it, but I'm happy that Raymond thought of you. If our mother was still alive she'd certainly be entitled to it." Because of the unknowns, Leo decided to delay talking to the others until he had the additional information that Raymond was sending. A few days later it arrived by registered mail. It was a detailed list of what Orville had at the time of his death and a copy of the death certificate. It seems he died of natural causes, whatever that meant. The listing had notes made by Raymond on it where he thought explanations were needed. The document read as follows:

Orville L. Trapp Estate
Coles County, Illinois

As submitted by court appointed administrator: Raymond Trapp as of Date of Death – February 1, 1962.

1. Checking Account – Oakland National Bank $ 635.00.2. Savings Account – Oakland National Bank $ 3,248.00.
3. Cash on hand – premises $ 768.00.
4. Contents safe deposit – Oakland National Bank, Series E. Bonds, current value $10,262.00.
5. 1958 four door Chevrolet Automobile - $1,800.00.
6. 10.5 Acres Land East Oakland Township with 5 room home $42,000.00.
7. 40 Acres Farm Land - Coles County IL. $84,000.00.
8. Personal effects and household furniture - $1,000.00.
9. Life Insurance Policy Proceeds - $10,000.00.

Total Estate Value $153,705.00.

Leo was shocked. For a man who had absolutely nothing at one time, this was a considerable accumulation. The handwritten notes Raymond had made explained part of it. The forty acres had been Hazel's land that Orville inherited upon her death. He could now start planning on how he would approach the brothers. He discussed his own feelings first with his wife. A fourth share wasn't something to sneeze at, but Leo had inklings that others needed it worse. He had a father and a mother and was sure that one day the dairy farm of his parents would be either his or his kids. He decided to package up copies of the inventory with a letter of explanation and mail them to the brothers and await their input. A few days later William called and expressed that he'd rather the three brothers share it. He didn't need it, and like Leo he thought maybe Eddie could use it more. After all, Eddie didn't have a second set of other parents in his life. The brothers' consensus after looking over the inventory was that they didn't want ownership of the land. They had no emotional ties to it anymore. Since Leo thought that Raymond would be fair, the brothers agreed to let Raymond take care of it as the courts had appointed him to do so. This decision was passed on to Raymond, along with one question for him: can there be something other than an equal distribution if the majority of the brothers agree?" Raymond thought so, but he would check with the judge.

Raymond vowed to himself that he would do the best for Frances' boys that he could. He'd been there in the beginning and knew all the history. It wasn't pretty, and he was happy to contribute something now, even if he couldn't over thirty years ago. He didn't make excuses for his brother all these years because Orville never made excuses himself. Orville felt he had failed them all, plain and simple. He carried that guilt to his grave. He never interfered in their lives because he didn't deserve them. He deserted them and he lost them. Two children had died and he felt at least partially responsible for that. Four children were lost to adoption and he felt totally responsible for that. They must all hate him and so would the son born after he left. He had been an alcoholic at one time and knew it. The only way he could survive was to leave them alone and try not to dwell on his past sins. Raymond and his brother had stayed close over the years, but Frances was never a topic they could talk about after Orville finally came back from his misguided travels. The only time he had Raymond contact Frances for him was to have her start divorce proceedings.

Orville didn't have a will. He had made no plans for his assets. It was Raymond that stepped up and told the courts of his sons and it was Raymond who would get them what they were entitled. The legal notifications were published in the paper advising any and all who might have a claim against the estate. This was the law. Legal descriptions of the land were detailed. In time Raymond would proceed with sales and/or auction notifications to sell the property. Even before that happened there was unusual activity and interest at the courthouse where the records were on file. Raymond had worked many years for the County Farm Bureau and was pretty knowledgeable about land values. The interest in the forty acres was pretty predictable, but it was the ten acres that had a couple of parties calling him prematurely trying to circumvent any sales or bidding for the property. The interest did not appear to be about the house. Raymond decided he would do some investigation himself and found that small plots of ground in the general area, mostly along the Big Embarrass, were being bought up the past three years. The interesting part of the other sales was that mineral rights were intact. He saw enough that he decided to delay the sale and see what happened. He was hoping that Orville's sons would not get in any hurry for the distribution. It might pay to slow the sales process down. He'd discuss it with Leo if necessary, but in the meantime he probably should proceed selling the forty acres and distribute the liquid assets. He had some good offers, which the court had already approved. Selling it now would answer the question of who was going to plant this year's crop. That would be one less headache for Raymond.

Chapter 15

❧❧

The Retirement

William and Ted had gotten back together again when both families went to VMI for Ted's father's retirement party. There were too many of them to travel in one auto, so they decided it would be boys in one car and girls in the other. This gave Ted and William quality visiting time. William began by telling Ted, "It looks like we'll be leaving you and Joyce before long." This was a shock to Ted. "We hate the idea of not being near you but we've decided our calling is to move on to other things. We're returning to the St. Louis area where we see a huge need that we feel called to work on. I'm still relatively young, forty-three, and I've been either a student or a minister in a church every since the war. We have loved to minister in white-collar suburbia all these years but have decided we need more. Even Molly wants to get back into nursing. There are neighborhoods out there in desperate condition. We'll probably live in or near Webster Groves, where the children will have the advantage of being close to their grandparents and good schools, but we see the need in the ghettos."

After hearing William out, Ted volunteered that their stay in the area might be short lived also. "My temporary assignment is a dead-end job closing a small base in nearby Maryland, which is supposed to be completed by January 1962. We'll be able to continue to live in Alexandria until then and I'll commute, but after that I'm sure my next assignment will not be in the area. There's a good possibility that I could end up at Fort Leavenworth, Kansas."

"Why would you want to do something that you're overqualified for and are not happy doing, Ted?" William asked. "They haven't treated you right."

Ted could only drop his head and reply, "I just have to be practical. I have less than four years before I can take early retirement and get a pension. I need to tough it out for my family's sake. I've loved the military and up until now I think I've made a worthwhile contribution. I'm not going to be given that chance again under the present circumstances. Even when I retire at forty-two I'm not sure what I'll be doing. I need to spend the next four years planning for that and find a new challenge for my life. I'm at a loss, but for now I'll take the assignments offered and do the best I can. At least the family won't have to relocate for a while."

Ted's mother's condition did affect the pomp and circumstances of the formal retirement proceedings. The color and the flash of the young cadets were impressive, and the dignitaries and alumni lauding the accomplishments and character of General James Wainright certainly helped, but the pall was still there. William reminisced with Ted's mother about the occasion years ago when she had perpetrated a fraud on her son when William had first come to visit; how for a day

Ted was left in the dark and thought William was a visiting chaplain friend of the general. She smiled at the memory. "That was a special time," she said. "I'm so happy that he's rediscovered all of his brothers. His dad and I will soon be gone and this will become even more important. Thank you for the difference you're making in his life." William sadly noted that this might well be their final conversation.

They stayed overnight in the mansion one last time before heading back. For the return trip, after hugs and goodbyes, each family got in their own car. William thought it might be a nice side trip to take the family to historic Williamsburg. The opportunity may never arise again and Ursey would like parts of it. It was the height of the tourist season, but all went well. For a while they managed to leave the cares of the world behind.

Ted and Joyce and their children had a quiet trip back to Alexandria. They discussed the Watson's family announcement and what they themselves would be facing over the next six months. It wasn't in either of their natures to just tread water, life was to precious too waste, but by prayer and pulling together they knew they'd get through this. They prayed for peace and guidance for them and the family. It had been difficult leaving his parents, knowing they would be two thousand miles away before the week was out. Soon they would be leaving Joyce's parents also. It was a time of major adjustments for everyone. Ted was so thankful he had this wife with uncommon strength and faith. She would see that the children made the adjustments with minimal trouble.

Chapter 16

❧❦

New Hope In Colorado

In the spring of 1962 Eddie and Barbara were very near bankruptcy. The town had lost thirty manufacturing jobs to the big city. The impact of the loss of a $200,000 in annual payroll on the small community made a big difference. The ripple effect reached Eddie and Barb and they were forced to close the bar. With the dram shop insurance that was mandatory for all bar operators and the liquor license going up the first of the year, its fate was sealed. This also put the poolroom in jeopardy. They had a mortgage on everything they owned, plus there wasn't any market for their commercial property to sell out and try a new avenue. Unless they could convert the bar and poolroom to a rental property, and then rent it, the future looked pretty bleak. Bankruptcy was just around the corner, and they were sick with that thought. Barb's family had helped all they could. Eddie had gotten free labor from them, but quite frankly Eddie could not see where the next mortgage payment for the business or the house was coming from. The bank was trying to cooperate within their boundaries and Eddie had no gripe with them, but it was all very frustrating and depressing. In desperation Eddie had gone to Denver seeking work that would warrant a move there. His experience was farming and food service and about all he could find were entry-level jobs that would not support his family. In desperation he called his Uncle Robert who had settled in Denver over forty years ago and to whom he had only visited with on the phone. He had disconnected from Eddie's mom and family many years ago and was now living in retirement with his wife. He was pleasant enough to Eddie on the phone, but not encouraging as far as giving him any leads or hope of finding meaningful work. He felt he was just out of the main stream and wouldn't be any help. He wished Eddie well. Eddie returned home very discouraged.

Eddie's spirits could not have been lower than they were the day he received a letter from Leo. He'd been feeling sorry for himself and wondering what he had done to deserve all of this and couldn't seem to find a break. "Why me, Lord?" had passed his lips more than once. They suspected that Barb was pregnant, which had been a joyful occasion before, but not this time. His one ray of hope was a temporary janitor's job at the high school until school was out. A friend had to break his leg for him to even have that much. He was fighting depression and losing the battle. Only Barb was keeping him grounded. In a way, he at times could be thankful for his father. When his thoughts ran to the idea of obliterating his senses with drink, he would stop short, remembering what Orville's drinking had done to his family.

The contents of the envelope just about floored him and he raced to the restaurant to share it with Barb. The possibility of receiving thirty to thirty-five thousand dollars from Orville Trapp's estate was mind-boggling and a dream come true. It might be six months before they'd get anything, but at least they had a glimmer of hope to look forward to. It wasn't the total answer, but when he took the notice to the bank, it was good enough for their friends there to give them a second mortgage on the business. That would do a lot toward tiding them over. That evening he and Barb held hands around the table with their children and thanked God for their good fortune. Someone was praying for them. Without the loan, the trip to Kansas City for Memorial Day could not happen. Also, they could start the planning for remodeling the building to separate the bar and pool hall for the purpose of renting it out. A local pharmacist had shown real interest there. This might make things work. The restaurant might be enough. It may not be enough now that another mouth to feed was on its way, which would limit Barb's workload, but it might. It lifted their spirits tremendously and gave them a fighting chance. Barb had been seriously concerned with the physical and mental strain she had seen in her husband. Even good men succumb to stress at times, and her husband already had his share for one lifetime.

Barb had watched each of her siblings, except for one brother, leaving for greener pastures. Some went off to the military and others to college, but none had returned. Cheyenne Wells just didn't have livelihoods for them. She missed them so much. They had not only been good brothers and sisters but best friends, too. They fought like cats and dogs and loved every minute of it. Her parents were aging and her father was in pretty serious condition and didn't have long. Barb found working full-time at the restaurant and raising two small children was a big task. Now another baby was growing inside her. She wanted to want the baby, but it was difficult in the circumstances. Eddie was concerned about her. His working a second job, although temporary, had put additional strain and burden on his wife also. This gift from Heaven eased the burden enough that they just might get their second wind.

As Memorial Day approached they were eagerly looking forward to getting away. Barb's brother and a friend were going to keep the restaurant open while they were gone. In fact, even though they couldn't afford it, they were going a day early to stop to visit the Eisenhower Museum and Library in Abilene. Then they were going to stay overnight in Lawrence where Kansas University is. From there it was just a short drive into Kansas City where they'd be meeting the family. William had made all the arrangements and they would stay overnight there. It would be a tough trip for the kids because they'd have to start early, but well worth it. They'd conserve on finances anyway they could.

Chapter 17

❧ ❧

New Watson Life

It was difficult for William and Molly to tell their friends, neighbors, and fellow church members of their decision to leave. They'd had a wonderful ten years and many were almost like family. They understood William's heart, though, and knew he would follow it where God led him to go. The house search in the St. Louis area was pretty much put in the hands of AJ, who had volunteered to help them out. He lined up several prospects and Molly and William had flown out to check them out. They decided on one located in Kirkwood, a neighboring community of Webster Groves. They had told AJ that they would like something comparable to their Falls Church home and he had done the rest. The house they chose wasn't available until the first of October, so they ended up storing their furniture and moving in with William's parents for a month so that Ursey could start school.

Because of the move it took considerable time for William to get organized. He worked with the area ministerial alliance to develop a plan of action and select a target for their outreach. He attended meetings in the neighborhood chosen, attended small churches there, and got to know the different storefront religious operations dotting the business area. He got to know community leaders and officials and was telling them all about what the Kathryn Foundation hoped to do to help the homeless and hungry in the area. He was finding disarray and lack of organization for addressing the neighborhood problems. He worked to pull different elements together for one unified effort. They knew there was a problem with the homeless on the streets, hungry children, and violence, but it would take united leadership to try and turn the tide. William and the Kathryn Foundation offered that leadership. William met with opposition from some city officials, religious organizations, and skeptics. Some felt it was a condemnation of what they were trying to do. Some saw it as a way to pull their flocks away from them by being the foundation of a new church. Some thought it was part of a scam to line someone's pockets with cash at the expense of the poor by taking donations and grants away from them. But there was also strong support from leaders in the area who knew and appreciated what the Watson family had done on the humanitarian front for decades in St. Louis. William's dad and brother had worked, largely behind the scenes, for the betterment of the area and some important people knew this and were eager to help the Kathryn Foundation organization. The Watsons appointed a twelve-person board for the foundation. Some members were from the targeted neighborhood and others were individuals who felt the same commitment as the Watsons.

Using family reputation and connections, an appeal was made for financing the Kathryn Foundation. The whole family covered the media and met with many benevolence groups in an effort to raise the funds to get the project off the ground and operating for at least six months. The effort was very successful and a plan was made to have a Thanksgiving awareness dinner and fellowship time in the very area they were to serve. Everyone was invited, especially all of the homeless and poor that they hoped to serve. They only had three short weeks to find a suitable building, plan a banquet, and line up a staff to prepare and serve the food, and it demanded a huge effort. The turnout exceeded their expectations and William felt they garnered goodwill and respect from some of the skeptics and critics. Over nine hundred people showed up for the event which was the kickoff for meals being served twice daily commencing the day after Thanksgiving. It taxed them to feed that many, but with alternative menus and backup plans the job got done, even though some of it had to be done in shifts. Speeches were kept to a minimum and the whole goal of awareness and good intent was successful. It was well received and several thousand dollars in donations were voluntarily given that day.

Early on the Kathryn Foundation hired a staff of six cooks and food handlers to form a nucleus of what they hoped would be a volunteer army of workers. The first day, the center fed seventy-five hungry people and by the middle of December the daily number had grown to over three hundred. There were no qualification criteria. If they showed up, they were fed. They encouraged everyone to wash up before eating and the obviously diseased and intoxicated people were given special treatment by seating them and serving them to avoid them being around the serving tables. They recruited some of the healthier looking attendees to spend an hour or so helping to serve and clean up. Other than that, there was no charge.

The hope was to make the people feel that this was their own project and to help them to find pride in it.

One of William's first acquaintances in the area was in one of the storefront churches. This was Brother Aaron, a large black lay preacher who truly had a servant's heart. He was volunteering and helping from the start and William quickly learned to rely on him as his backup and grew to trust him totally. Because William couldn't always be there, he needed someone, and he had found him. The administrative chores and fundraising had to be done and the only one available for those tasks at the time was William himself. His parents would have liked to help, but their health prohibited their active participation. The initial financing campaign had done great, but no one anticipated the impact and immediate need. Plus, this was just step one in the outreach plan. They still had the homeless to shelter and the sick to treat.

Ten days before Christmas Brother Aaron called William at home. He told him that the Department of Health had just closed the doors and people were outside waiting to be fed. William and Molly quickly bundled the children up, took them to their grandparents, and made a beeline for the center thirty minutes away. When they arrived the health inspector was just finalizing his list and giving a copy to Brother Aaron. William immediately appealed to his humanitarian senses to allow them to use the prepared food to feed the people waiting. The man wouldn't listen and his response was littered with bureaucratic mumbo-jumbo. William looked at the violations. Many would take months to fix. He decided that this was a time for civil disobedience. He called the mayor, who in turn sent the police over to open the doors. Despite warnings of retribution and fines, the hungry were fed. William immediately got on the phone with a supporter that he had met before the foundation was formed. The Bishop of the Greater St. Louis Catholic Church heard him out and then made some calls of his own. His first call to the mayor of St. Louis, plus the call to the bishop, led to a call to the governor who wasted no time in calling off the bureaucrats in the Department of Health. The next day they were feeding as usual with a promise that a committee was working to correct the violations. William had known, as everyone else had, that the conditions weren't right, but the immediate need outweighed the waiting for things to be one hundred percent. He was doubtful that anyone could ever do all that the bureaucrats wrote up as regulations.

Because this created a new concentration of people at a given time of day, it was soon decided that security would be needed also. A security force was set up of off-duty policemen who worked well below the scale that they were accustomed. Two bad instances, one involving William, had highlighted the need. A group of thugs, or gangs as they chose to be known as, had come in bullying the patrons and stealing equipment and canned goods. When William confronted them he was beaten and kicked, but escaped any severe damage when the police arrived to handle the situation. The security was to minimize this type of problem. This was a difficult lesson for William, who chose to think the best of everyone.

The enormity of the task so engulfed William that he encouraged Molly to minimize her involvement so that the children would not be neglected. Christmas came and went and William hardly noticed as there were demands on his time seven days a week, and they fed the hungry on Christmas. That reminded William that they had not even begun to feed the souls of these people yet. But he knew he was doing what Jesus would have done. Take care of their needs first and the rest will follow. He took no salary from the foundation and vowed he would not for the first year. The family had what they needed and all that was raised was put to the use it was raised for. He did put Brother Aaron on the payroll at the first of the year, as he was spending more and more time on the job and William needed the backup. He was lucky to have him.

Although he exchanged several calls with Leo and had talked once or twice to the other brothers, William was pretty focused on his main concerns at this point, his family and the Kathryn Foundation. People around him marveled that this man with his doctorate and potential to fill about any pulpit in the nation was doing what he was doing. One day he would be meeting with government officials at the capitol, and the next he could be seen mopping floors at the center. Often, when it was bedtime, he'd be bone tired, but his last conscious thoughts were of thanksgiving. He was being fulfilled. This was the same experience he had as a chaplain during the war in the front lines of Europe. He now had one major supporter at hand that he didn't have then, a loving wife. Molly understood her man and was always there for him, although sometimes she had to urge him to pace himself for the long run. By Memorial Day he hoped that the organization would be working better. He knew he would need recharging, and meeting with his brothers would be the way he would choose to do so. He was looking forward to Kansas City and the brothers. There would be just the four families this year.

Chapter 18

❧ ❦

Ted's Final Command

The Army Post, founded in 1827 on the Missouri River, and the daily routine could not have been more different than anything Ted had experienced in his army life. After years of four lane highways and massive military compounds, the biggest being the Pentagon, Ted, Joyce, and family arrived at Fort Leavenworth, Kansas, the second week of January 1962. Ted was ready for the change; the past four months had been totally unfulfilling and boring. His job of putting the final nails into the base that Congress and the Pentagon had deemed expendable was definitely one for an officer the Army had deemed expendable. He had a total of 50 staff members to complete the project, making sure everything was packed, moved, or boarded and sealed up. He was thankful it was over.

When he was finally reassigned to Fort Leavenworth, he knew the adjustment for both he and the family would be a major one. Located just fifty miles north of Kansas City, Kansas, this was the oldest fort west of the Mississippi. It had been on the route of the original Lewis and Clark Trail and the earliest outpost to protect the wagon trains from the Indians. It was the jumping off point for many going to the Santa Fe or Oregon/California Trails. The fort originally set right on the riverbank, but time had shifted the river and rerouted it some distance away. The fort itself was named for Colonel Henry Leavenworth, a veteran of the War of 1812 who is buried there. The compound consists of a thousand buildings and fifteen hundred living quarters for personnel assigned there. Ted was assigned one of the homes reserved for senior officers. They had put their home in Virginia up for sale, as it was highly unlikely that they'd ever be returning to either the Pentagon or the D.C. area. Their new home was actually larger than the one they had lived in for the past ten years.

Ted's new assignment was as executive officer in charge of the College for General Staff Training. The post had evolved from an outpost to the largest disciplinary barracks in the army. It was a prison, and that was its main purpose. Ted, being a part of the Army Command School, was not directly involved with the prison and he was very happy about that. William T. Sherman, the general who burned Atlanta, established the College in 1881. Before World War II, it had trained the likes of Eisenhower, Bradley, and Patton. It also has one of the first National Cemeteries that Abraham Lincoln had established in 1862. The first Protestant chapel was built by prison labor in 1878. The head chaplain of the post was Ted's new neighbor.

Acclimating to the new job was difficult for Ted. It was so unlike anything he had ever done in the past, but fortunately he himself was only twelve years from the academic setting of West Point and that was helpful. The students were staff officers being posted there for only about six months at a time, and not cadets, so his job was to develop an ever-changing curriculum for an ever-changing world. The Army had recognized that he had combat experience and wanted to draw on that experience. He wasn't the general making the decision on D-Day or in charge of the plans for carrying the battle to German soil, but as a lieutenant he had more experience than most in leading troops in combat. Training leaders for the next war in the nuclear age was much different, however, and would require a broad scope of tactics be explored. He was uniquely qualified for the job.

He felt fortunate that he wasn't directly involved with the prison. Part of his command did offer classes for the inmates, but that was an assignment relegated to junior officers and non-commissioned officers. The prisoners were from all walks of life and of all ages that had experienced problems while in the military. Some were there for a few years and others for life. It was a depressing place. Ted couldn't help but wonder how many of these men were innocents railroaded by army justice where commanders managed to pass the buck. He knew from experience that happened. His knowledge of the prison was from his fellow officers that he lived near and socialized with. In that respect, an army post was always like a big fraternity. The chaplain was very much involved with the prisoners and Ted probably heard more about the place than he really wanted to. The men inside didn't have much hope and that's a depressing thing to encounter day after day. It takes a special person to cope with that atmosphere.

Joyce was surprised by how much she was enjoying her new home. Her husband had a nine to five job and was home every night. They had nice neighbors with young children for her kids to play with. Jimmy and Casey were adapting very well. She was also getting deeply involved with the church, much to the delight of the chaplain and his wife. They had found a willing and excellent worker in her. If her husband had not been so conflicted she could have been totally happy here. Her own father had moved them from base to base as she was growing up and her mother had coped and made the best of it. Joyce had learned a lot from her.

The unanswered question before Joyce and Ted was what were they going to do when this was over? They could serve until Ted had his twenty years in here, but at age forty-two, what would they do then? They weren't the type of people that could just get by. They needed to contribute in a real way. They prayed a lot about that.

They missed Molly and William very much and were looking forward to the Memorial Day meeting. Things had just not worked out to meet with them on their move because of William's busy schedule. Once things were organized, maybe they would have time for more visiting. They had stayed abreast of his progress and were praying for him in what seemed like an endless task. Who would have thought that things could change so much in the last year. Now virtually all the brothers would be within a day's drive of each other, with the exception of Eddie and Leo. Circumstances, or was it prayer, seemed to be drawing them closer together. Leavenworth was only about five hundred miles from Leo or Eddie and even closer to William. They were all still relatively young men, Leo being the oldest. Who was to say they wouldn't have a normal relationship after all? When they got settled into their new surroundings, they could start making those trips. They still would need to fly to see Ted and Joyce's parents, but the brothers would be closer.

Chapter 19

❧❧

Kansas City Meeting

Although they had stayed at Lawrence the night before and were very close, Eddie and Barb had been the last to arrive at the Kansas City motel. Something of interest had come up in Lawrence that morning and they took the time to explore it. They loved the looks of the college town and fully agreed that one day they would love to live in Lawrence. That's what they had taken the time to do. They looked at a restaurant advertised for sale. They knew they couldn't touch it financially, but they checked it out anyway. It was their dream.

After registering at the motel, he returned to his car and laughingly told Barb of the look he got from the clerk behind the desk. "I originally gave him my name and the man was having troubles finding the reservation. I mentioned my brother William Watson might have put it in his name. The man looked and found four rooms reserved in the east wing, all right together. He asked if we were business associates and I told him no, we're brothers. He looked a little perplexed.

I volunteered that we were all blood brothers, with the same mother and father, and that we were separated early in life. Some were adopted but that was a long story that he wouldn't care to hear. He indicated the others had already checked in but that he'd like to hear my story sometime. He said it would probably be more interesting that most of the stories that crossed the registration desk."

Before long the four families were going from one room to the next in an open door policy. The kids thought the hallways were their private playgrounds. Fortunately, it was still early in the day and most of the rooms weren't occupied yet. The private dining area wasn't quite as nice as the setup in Terre Haute, but adequate for some privacy. They had their rooms to retire to for the evening for visiting, which they did non-stop. Finally, they put the kids down together in one room until they were ready for bed, which wasn't until near midnight. They took off their shoes and really made an evening of it. Someone had brought cards, but they never quite got around to playing. Everyone was thrilled to hear of Barb's pregnancy and wanted to know the name selected and she told them it was still pending. Any one of the ladies would have gladly traded places with her. They milled around from room to room, with nothing planned but just talk. After the kids were in bed, they all congregated together for the rest of the evening. They had a lot to learn of each other, especially Leo and Carol. The men had discussed the inheritance and how shocked they were to hear of it. Leo brought them up to date on Raymond's last phone call. He said some developments had happened that didn't affect the estate, but possibly the length of time that it was going to take to settle it. "He didn't elaborate," Leo said. Eddie did question when Leo thought things might be settled, but Leo couldn't say for sure. "He might do a partial distribution in August or September, but we'll just have to wait and see."

Ted told them all of his dilemma and what had happened since their last meeting. He got pretty discouraged telling it, but they all encouraged him and worked to lift his spirits. Basically, their opinion was that Ted could do anything he set his heart on. He had already proven that. In the end, Ted was feeling better.

William's undertaking was mind-boggling. All they could do was admire the effort he was making as William himself admitted he was overwhelmed at the task before him and his associates. "I have to look at the small victories," he said. "I can't look at the needs of thousands and say woe is me. I have to look at one more being fed and thinking, I'll help feed another one tomorrow. At least we made a difference for that one."

Leo had a happy story. He just wanted to thank his brothers for not giving up on him. Until the cloud of his adoption had been lifted, he had carried resentment and bitterness around in his heart and it affected him. He didn't know how badly it had affected him until he started seeing the consequences in his own son. This past year had worked miracles for him and his family and a big burden had been lifted. His family was truly whole, probably for the first time ever. As he had changed, he and Carol had seen the change in their son also.

Eddie was the quietest of the group and they had to draw him out. Only after leading questions, that only brothers can ask, did he explain the business climate at home and the affect it was having on their lives. They all listened closely with interest and Eddie tried to put a positive bend to it. Pride would not allow himself to tell the whole truth that he was close to failure. He couldn't have them believe that their younger brother was a failure after they had done so well.

Eddie did open up during the course of the day about his upbringing. It wasn't something that he had reason to be ashamed of, but he had hidden it from his mom for years and he had no reason to tell until he felt really close to his brothers. He had told his wife before they married, and now he explained his resentment of the Knight family to his brothers. Although they had given his mom employment for years, they had managed to make Eddie feel less than them. This made a lasting mark on a young boy growing up. Leo and William said they noted his resistance to talk of them when they had visited Coles County and thought it peculiar that he hadn't made it a point to visit the home where he lived all of his life before moving out west. William assured Eddie that his reaction was pretty normal for a child and young man who had to grow up in the conditions he had faced. Yes, his mom was a positive force, but the other authority figures in his life tended to belittle his self-esteem by making him feel worthless or by physically mistreating him. By doing so they stole a part of his childhood and he resented it. It had taken maturity to finally succeed in putting that life behind him. He was to be commended.

Not all conversations were in groups. They singled each other out for one-on-ones and intermingled with spouses and children during the entire day. It was like a hunger to know and understand each other. "Is this the case in all families," Leo asked, "Or is this just because of our special circumstances?"

Ted offered that most families had fifteen to twenty years of close living and didn't need the intensive bonding. Eddie said, "Maybe it's because Mom would have wanted us to."

The kids were a special joy to watch. Although William was the oldest child, Katie seemed to be the leader of the pack. She was the more aggressive and outgoing and the younger ones loved her. Some of the little ones had similar personalities and would have given her a run for her money had they been a little older, but they all got on well. Rudy was probably the rowdiest and most physical. The toddlers Casey and little Art played very well together and Debby was a little mother to them.

Ted, Leo, and William were up early the next morning and met at the coffee shop before the others got up. Their conversation quickly turned to the inheritance and what they wanted done. Despite William's encouraging them to split it among themselves, as he didn't need it, they all wanted Eddie to have it. They were all relatively secure themselves and could see that Eddie would make the best use of it. It really got down to the question of what Mom would have wanted them to do. They all came up with the same answer. God had furnished them stable and loving homes and parents in addition to their mother's heritage. Eddie had Mom too, but he never got the family support needed for a successful start in life. He never had a chance for more education or the environment they had each experienced. Hopefully, receiving this kind of a shot in the arm would help him and Barb at this time and not hurt them. They had to trust their instincts that it would. $130,000 may not alleviate the pain and abuse he had encountered growing up, but it could show their regard for him and their desire to see him succeed. Leo said he would handle the details with Raymond and get back to them. He knew they were making the right decision. About that time Eddie showed up for breakfast with the rest of the families smiling and joking and ready for a new day.

The pool was open after breakfast and all the families met there to swim and or watch the kids. It was a relaxed and joyful morning. They would have liked to stay longer, but some of them had timetables and responsibilities to meet. After lunch Leo and family were ready to leave for a Rocky Mountain vacation and Eddie's bunch started their long trip back to Colorado. They had some pretty pressing business to take care of there. The reunion had been all they had hoped it would be and individually they had made plans to visit each other's homes in the near future.

William and Ted weren't in any hurry to leave. In fact, William had his room for an extra night. He needed the extra time away. The four of them talked at length about the challenges they were facing and something was said that reminded William of the dream he'd had before the first reunion in Terre Haute. "You remember that dream I told you about when you woke me the morning we drove to Terre Haute, dear?" William asked Molly. She acknowledged she did. He went on to tell Joyce and Ted about the dream where their mom, grandparents, Orvie, Art and Ursie were observing the boys at Art's gravesite. "It was a special feeling and I woke up when my wife shook me, wishing it would go on and on. Last night I dreamed that Mom asked me if I thought Art would have been a preacher had he lived? I just said I didn't know. She said, 'Funny, but I always thought two of my sons would be ministers.' I'm always dreaming, but these were special. Most I don't remember very long, but these two I will." Ted sat listening quietly for a moment thinking of William's dreams. A simple story, but it was having a strange impact on him.

Chapter 20

৵৽

A Move of Faith

The kids had never been happier than the week they spent at Estes Park in Colorado. They were old enough to do limited exploring on their own and the shallow streams and woods around their cabin were beautiful. For Carol and Leo it was the most relaxed and wonderful time they had ever experienced on vacation. Although they were inexperienced, they rented the equipment and vowed to learn to fish using casting rods. They had limited success, so their fish dinners were purchased at the market. They hated to leave at the end of the week, but all good things must end and they started back via the northern route. They had seen enough of Kansas and this time they saw Wyoming and the Dakotas. Being confined in an auto for two days with their children gave them the chance to hear all their dreams and aspirations. Some they heard several times over. William liked to sleep a lot when the car was moving, but Katie had endless stories and her energy exhausted them. Where she got her fire, nobody knew. She was still so young but had definite ideas of what she wanted to do and serving God was at the top of her list. Carol thought to herself, "At age nine I was only interested in playing with dolls."

Leo didn't waste any time contacting Raymond once they were home. He informed him of the brothers' decision on the estate. Raymond told him to obtain the affidavits from the brothers to convey their rights to Eddie. Once he had those in hand he could proceed. It was at this time that Raymond confided in Leo that he had decided not to liquidate the home place where Orville had lived. Prospective buyers had already offered him more than he had anticipated and Raymond thought that possibly it might be a good idea just to hold on to the property and find out why it was in such demand. That decision had been made simpler now that it could be conveyed to just one brother by deed instead of a four way split. Eddie could decide at some future date what he wished to do about it. "If I get the releases back in the next thirty days," Raymond said, "I think we can have this wrapped up by fall."

Katie, meanwhile was developing a new love in her life. She'd been introduced to ice skating by a friend the past winter and couldn't get enough of it. Apparently she was a natural. Just north of Rockford was a year round ice rink and she talked them into taking her there often so she could practice. It wasn't unusual for her to want to spend all day Saturday there. After the Swenson's got to know the management, sometimes they'd drop her off and pick her up five or six hours later. Some weeks she'd find friends going and could car-pool. The owners did take an interest in her and encouraged her and gave her tips. During the summer she wanted to skate everyday, but that wasn't possible. Before long, Mrs. Kinsey, the owner suggested that they should find a coach for Katie, as she was a serious talent with the interest to match that could result in her becoming a class figure skater. With that encouragement they started off with rental training films and then progressed on to correspondence with professional coaches. They actually met and talked with a visiting coach who was a friend of the Kinsey's. She observed Katie and verified what Mrs. Kinsey had said. More importantly, Katie was having fun with it. They would have ice reviews and contests and before long Katie was the star performer leading various productions. If she was this good by age nine, her potential by fifteen seemed to be limitless as long as she loved it and worked at it diligently.

Leo had never been demonstrable about his Christian beliefs, although he'd been very faithful about joining his family each week for services. About six years before he was asked to serve as a deacon for his congregation and declined, feeling he wasn't ready for that. Recently the minister and elders had approached him again. With training and encouragement, he accepted. He was forty-five and felt the need for a deeper commitment. He was also sensing a change in Carol. She had not been raised in a Christian family, but had been content to attend church with Leo. Her father and mother believed there was a God, but were not convinced that Jesus was anything other than a teacher and good man. They didn't condemn the church, but didn't feel a need for it. Their church was nature and the universe, and they could pray to God in that way without getting committed to an institution. They had a Bible, but rarely opened it. Carol's only experience and teaching growing up was from her association with friends. Some were Jewish, some Catholic, and some attended several different denominational Protestant churches. Her exposure came when she would occasionally go with a friend for social reasons, and as a teen she attended a Bible School Camp a couple of times with girlfriends. The experience awakened her curiosity, but the home influence was stronger, until Leo came along. They met and fell in love and she could tell that this man was a true believer. She loved the man, and so church became a way of life with her also. It wasn't until the children were born that she began to get truly serious about what she was hearing and learning. She learned along with the kids and her commitment had grown every year until she knew that she also needed to be baptized and dedicate her life. She truly felt that sharing a Christian life with Leo and the children was a marvelous turning point in her life and she encouraged Leo in his leadership role. Seeing his commitment and finding the same in his brothers lives was so remarkable to Carol. Here were four men that basically only had one thing in common, their mother, and all four had grown up to be good, believing, Christian men. No one had to convince Carol of the power of a mother's prayer. She was finding that prayer in her own life was a very rewarding experience.

William had an unexpected growth spurt just before entering high school and he just loved the idea of looking down on his dad. He also loved the idea of being able to compete better on the basketball court. That was his passion. He developed new confidence in himself and was developing into a fine young man. Seeing his Uncle William, who was a head taller than any of his brothers, encouraged him, and he hoped to continue growing. He couldn't wait for school to start so that he could show off his newfound rebounding ability and hopefully make the basketball squad.

Chapter 21

৵৽

Manna From Heaven

The remodeling of the building separating the restaurant from the bar and poolroom had taken every cent that Eddie could scrounge. On September 1st he received his first rental check from the pharmacist, which was sufficient to make the overdue mortgage payment. Although the lessee would only commit to a one-year contract, that one year gave Barb and him a little breathing room. Now he just needed to make enough to feed his family and pay his own bills. The bank would get theirs from the rental payment. They still didn't have an answer for the additional bills coming with the baby in November.

Eddie was working long hours. He insisted that Barb get off her feet as much as possible the last three months of her pregnancy. She was secretly hoping it wasn't twins. She felt so big. She had been feeling good all along and she thanked God for that. The hours were long, and trying to keep up with the family and the restaurant left her exhausted each evening. The heat didn't bother her as badly as it did

Eddie. This was all she ever knew, but Eddie suffered. She wished they could afford a window air conditioner for their bedroom so he could sleep better. The children were looking forward to a new baby. Of course, Debby wanted a baby sister, and Rudy a brother. They'd almost come to blows over that argument. Barb had been one of eight children herself and loved large families. It was getting a little late to count on a large family, but three would be just great. She worried some about giving them enough time and attention with the workload. One advantage of small town living was the fact that you could always be close even when you were at work. The grandparents were right there within walking distance, the streets were relatively secure and safe, and the children were old enough to walk to the restaurant anytime they wanted. It could be a lot worse. From time to time she would get a gentle reminder of a foot in her abdomen.

Eddie was walking home after the noon lunch hour and cleanup to take care of a chore he had been putting off. He was handy enough with tools, but finding the time and the strength was the problem. There were always things needing repairs around the restaurant and the house and he had developed into a jack-of-all-trades by necessity. He couldn't afford a plumber or an electrician every time something went wrong. His handyman book that Barb had gotten him for Christmas was his reading material. Once in a while he'd get to read a paperback western. As he approached the house he heard his name being called and turned to see Marty the postmaster approaching him. "I have a registered letter here Eddie. It just came and I'd seen you walk by so I followed you to get you to sign for it." Eddie took the large envelope from him and thanked him. Going into the house he sat at the table and opened the envelope. It was from Raymond.

His hands shook as he anticipated what might be inside. He took out several items, some stapled together and others loose, and spread them across the table. He read Raymond's cover letter, which said:

Enclosed are the following:

1. A Cashier's Check drawn on the Charleston First State Bank for $114,562.00. This is the total cash proceeds of the Orville Trapp Estate from all sources.

2. The Deed for 10.5 Acres of land consisting of a five-room house located in East Oakland Township. (The home place in Canaan)

3. A copy of my accounting to the courts for all business pertaining to my administration of the estate.

His head was swimming as he read on. The letter said that his brothers, the other heirs to the estate, had relinquished all rights and privileges to the estate and its assets in favor of him. This was done legally and approved by the courts and was irreversible. The court had accepted this final report and the liquidation terms and had released Raymond of all my duties and responsibilities under the order.

In the final paragraph Raymond told him the house was currently rented on a month-to-month basis to a Ben Marchant. Mr. Marchant was willing to enter into a lease agreement for three years with Eddie at the current rate if Eddie chose to do so. A copy of the proposed lease was enclosed, and if Eddie approved, Raymond would be happy to act as go between, or whatever arrangement he preferred. He would explain to Eddie in a letter following of reasons he had for not liquidating the ten-acre property.

Eddie sat absolutely stunned, disbelieving this windfall, and reread the documents in front of him again. What had these brothers done? The one-quarter share that he had come to anticipate had been too good to be true, but this surpassed his wildest dreams. He was limp as he got to his feet. The rear porch door would just have to hang by one hinge for another day. His knees were physically weak. Talk about brotherly love. How could he ever repay them? He started up the street, slowly regaining his energy until he ended jogging all the way to the restaurant, which he entered, winded and sweating. Barb was sitting in the back booth with her feet up reading a favorite magazine. She looked up as he came huffing in, wondering what his rush was. "Sit down," he said.

"I already am, ding dong, it looks like you'd better be the one to sit before you blow a fuse," she replied. "What's going on?" She moved her feet so he could sit facing her. He sat there shaking and with tears in his eyes. He took both of her hands in his, and by the end of the story there were two adults sitting and gazing in each other's eyes with tears streaming down their faces. Puddles were starting to form on the plastic tabletop. A customer came in after a while, and broke the trance, but they were so stunned that the service they gave him was not very good. Fortunately, he was an old friend and would be forgiving.

Other than banking the check, they did nothing for a week. It was a week given to prayer and thanksgiving as each brother was called, but at the end of the week Eddie sent the approved land lease back to Raymond and had contacted the realtor in Lawrence, Kansas to see if the restaurant they had looked at over Memorial Day was still on the market. Happily they found it still was and the negotiations began.

The $75,000 down payment was enough to get the necessary bank financing to purchase the restaurant. Because of the baby being so near, the closing date was postponed until the first of December. This would give Eddie the time to do what he wanted to do in the way of remodeling by January. That would be their grand opening. Barb and Eddie thought long and hard before they came up with a name for their new restaurant. The name that stuck was the comment Barb's mother had made when she learned of their good fortune. She said, "What a blessing for you kids." Blessings was the name they chose. It was in an ideal location, not on campus, but near enough to get some of that business as well as the townspeople.

More blessings were on their way. All of this was made the more perfect when their baby daughter was born on November 8th, in perfect health. What a difference a year can make. This daughter, which Barb wasn't sure they could afford six months ago, was now one of the happiest occasions of their lives. Blessings came in all sizes and shapes. They finally settled on the name Ruby. That was Eddie's idea. Being warned of the confusion of having a Ruby and a Rudy did not dissuade him. He insisted that he had so many jewels in his crown, from his mom on down, and this was just another jewel, a Ruby. He thanked God everyday for this change in their lives and told anyone who would listen that he had a prayer warrior in Heaven, and she had been praying for him everyday of his life. Even on the difficult ones.

The day after Christmas, Eddie and Barb and family moved to a modest home in Lawrence, which did have air conditioning. Their Cheyenne Wells home had a prospective buyer, and Barb's younger brother wanted to try his hand at the restaurant business, so they worked out a deal with him. The move was uneventful as the weather held and the Trapp family saw the New Year begin, in their new home. What a marvelous year it had been. These past two years with the brothers and other happenings had done a lot to help them forget about the really tough years. Eddie felt an obligation to his brothers to succeed in being a good steward of their gift, but also to be the man that their mom had prayed he would be. He didn't think of Art often, the brother he had never met, but somehow he felt so close now to this young man who had died so young. In a way he thought of himself as a substitute brother for the one who couldn't be reunited. His surviving brothers couldn't do for Art, so instead they had done this wonderful thing for him and his family. It was a special feeling.

Eddie had hired a new staff for the restaurant and on January 2nd they were open for business. The "Blessings" was in business and the Trapp's were operating at a new level that Eddie had only dreamed of. This one was five times larger than the one they left behind in Cheyenne Wells. He expanded his menu and became the chef he always wanted to be. "Down home cooking like Mom used to make" was his advertising motto. "Good Food and Lots of It" was on the marquee.

Chapter 22

❧❧

Foundation At Work

The best laid plans of mice and men was the old adage William was thinking about as he listened to the discussions of the foundation trustees. Their plan had been to secure a location that was accessible to the people, large enough to serve the people, and expandable so services could grow as the resources were provided. The area selected was in north St. Louis City, in an area near where the pride of St. Louis, the Cardinals, had just vacated for a downtown location. A new stadium downtown replaced Old Sportsman Park in the north end, and now the park was in a state of decay. There were many abandoned buildings and businesses and the surrounding housing had deteriorated almost to the point of no return. Many people had lost hope as they saw their properties decaying. All of the foundation's efforts were pointed to one goal, and that was to aid the people of the neighborhood. They encouraged the formation of unity groups so that neighbor could help neighbor pull themselves up by the bootstraps, but also to help reclaim some neighborhood pride. Encouraging to William was the fact that these groups were now being formed and one in particular had by-laws and purpose statements to guide their efforts. One such by-law stated: "We exist to promote and create a viable productive and conducive living environment for our residents through continued neighborhood stabilization." William admired that. Their motto was: "If It's To Be, It's Up To Me." The Kathryn Foundation applauded them for the positive steps they were taking and was ready to help. The people were working to improve the situation.

The foundation had found a closed up furniture store that they thought could be resurrected for the purpose of feeding, housing, and other services. It had two stories and adequate wiring and plumbing that could be fixed in a short time so that the feeding of the hungry would not be unduly delayed. That they accomplished. As the numbers grew they added more shifts to feed the people. Stage two was the plan to make temporary housing available as money became available. The upstairs would be utilized, with the dining area on the ground floor being used for overflow on any given night. All housing was to be of a temporary nature to get the people out of the elements and off the streets. The third stage would be a medical unit in the north end of the structure. Because the first stage of feeding the people had so exceeded their projections, the other stages were on hold because of the lack of funding. Brother Aaron was just explaining the latest round with the Health Department to the trustees assembled. "Much work has been done to correct the code violations," he said, "but by trying to offer housing before the cold weather hits, the Health Department has taken the position that the wiring, while adequate for feeding, is not adequate for sleeping. They also said the bathroom situation is inadequate and they will not allow housing people until improvements are made in all areas. The committee is working hard on all of these complaints so we can get waivers, but it looks unlikely that the shelter will be ready by Thanksgiving or before cold weather hits." This report lit a fire under the trustees and they redoubled their efforts. As spokesman, chief financial officer, and overall manager, there were nights when William didn't make it home. He was often so exhausted that when the last person was fed, he'd curl up right there and sleep a few hours before the demands of a new day started. He had quickly learned that administration at this level took special talent and he envied Ted's expertise in this area. He wished he had more.

On a day in October his brother AJ called and set up a luncheon date with him. William had neglected him in this busy time and was looking forward to seeing him. He was surprised when he arrived to see his dad with AJ. He was delighted that he felt well enough to be out and around and they enjoyed their lunch together. His dad spoke up when they had finished. "William, I couldn't be prouder of what you are doing and what you have accomplished. It's been needed for a long time, and the fact that you've set up this Christian foundation to do it is the right way of doing it. If Christians had always been as unselfish and caring, the national welfare state would not be in the shape it's in today. There is one criticism, and I hope you'll accept it the way it's intended. It comes from both your brother and I who have been there and done it. Not to the degree you are, but we understand your plight. You need to set boundaries. You know you have limitations, but you haven't adequately defined your boundaries. The federal government has the power of the treasury and it can't solve the problem. The state and city governments, with the ability to tax, cannot solve the problem. And you and the foundation cannot solve the problem. What you can do is make a difference. Unless you set your boundaries, you're taking the chance of failing in the long run. You and your associates need to set realistic goals and stay within your resource base. You started with a good plan, but demands have you changing the goals. The boundaries are getting skewed. Yesterday you fed twelve hundred people. To do so you cut corners. Next month you will not be able to offer shelter to the homeless because you're trying to feed the world. You need to establish real priorities and work the plan. Establish a plan to take care of the truly needy and not the greedy who are now taking advantage of your organization." William listened to this wisdom from the man he most admired in this world. How could he not? His dad had one last comment. "And above all, don't neglect your family. Promise me you won't do that. It is God's will that you take care of your family, first and foremost." AJ offered some practical suggestions before William returned to the Center. William knew he needed to take some time to pray and think over the situation at hand. He needed guidance and he'd been neglecting the one with the answers.

The next morning he and Brother Aaron got the foundation advisors together and seriously discussed a new plan of action for the Center. The criteria they agreed upon would certainly create some displeasure in the clientele and providers alike, but the ones they continued to serve would be better served, and hopefully they would be the ones who needed it the most.

By Thanksgiving they did have temporary housing for over fifty people. Over the next two years their facility was capable of feeding two thousand a day, had temporary shelters for one hundred and twenty five, and a full time nurse on staff with a schedule of doctors volunteering their time. They were fulfilling their purpose. The Kathryn Foundation received recognition by the city and state for their humanitarian efforts and the local ministerial alliance used their plans and their success to help others start centers in other parts of the city. The foundation continued working hand in hand with other organizations to reach the unwed mothers and those dealing with alcohol and drug abuse. The trustees were also working closely with an evangelistic organization to open another facility in the Linwood area.

At this time William decided it was time for him to step out of the active day to day management. There was a nucleus of personnel doing a wonderful job, led by Brother Aaron, and he felt it was time for him to move on. He would remain on the board and continue to be a prominent fundraiser because he would never lose his love for the cause, but he missed and wanted to return to the pulpit ministry. When he was contacted about a position in Kirkwood, he and Molly looked it over and decided it would be a good fit for them. The day he announced it to the other trustees they weren't too surprised and quickly approved his recommendation to appoint Brother Aaron to take his place. What surprised them most was when they discovered Brother Aaron's real name. There in black and white on the announcements that the Kathryn Foundation would have a new chairman was the name, Brotherly Aaron Love. Brotherly Love. Who better to lead the foundation? His mother must have been a prophet.

In the months following, the Watsons were all honored for their humanitarian efforts. Mr. and Mrs. Watson died in that period of time, within six months of each other, which was a tremendous loss to the family and the many they had befriended. They didn't suffer, which William was thankful for. His mother died of pneumonia in her sleep and just months later his dad died of heart failure. The real legacy of Charles and Kathryn Watson was the impact they had made on lives, including family, for over fifty years in their community. The family knew Dad had died out of loneliness for his beloved wife, but that couldn't be put down on any legal document. In their will they provided a legacy for the Kathryn Foundation that would insure financial aid to the organization for years to come. AJ and William vowed to carry on the family tradition of helping others.

At AJ's encouragement, William and Molly moved into his parent's home that they had always loved so much in Webster Groves. It was a constant reminder of his parents, and that was painful at times, but the home also reminded William of their warmth and love. This was where William and Molly raised Ursey and Charles Arthur much as he had been raised. This is where they held family reunions for the brothers and introduced them all to their beloved Cardinals and the Muni-Opera House. This was where their children would be educated and taught the values that his parents had instilled in him. This is where Molly and William prayed each day for their children and family, much as Frances had prayed for them. They had come home. Now William had three prayer warriors in Heaven looking out for him and the family.

Chapter 23

❧❧

A New Calling

Ted was doing all he could to make a difference at Leavenworth. New challenges were facing the military and the command college was attempting to keep abreast by adapting new strategies demanded by the changing world. President Kennedy had warned in 1961 of the impending challenge by the communists in Southeast Asia. Some one had coined the phrase "domino affect," meaning if one country fell to communism, the next country would also fall as lined up dominos would. There were already hundreds of advisors in Viet Nam trying to help the nationals stem the tide there. The average American didn't even know of a country called Viet Nam. Few equated it with Indo-china and the turmoil the French had there for a decade. Many maps of the world didn't even show a Viet Nam. Like Korea, the country had been split in the middle with the communists controlling the north and the nationals the south.

The family had adjusted and was comfortable and happy. They were very involved in church and Joyce had several other organizations seeking her participation, but her church came first. Ted's friendship with Gene was growing and becoming very important to him. Gene, the post's head chaplain, was a little older than Ted, and was athletic and very dedicated to his chosen field. In ways they were much alike. Lately their conversation was more and more about the Bible and discussions were getting longer and more intense. Ted was hungry to learn. He had never been a student of the Bible and was soaking up Gene's knowledge like a sponge. They even started a weekly Bible study with other men to get a greater cross section of input and it caught on well. Apparently it wasn't only Ted looking for a deeper meaning to life. They had to split into two groups so that everyone would have a chance to participate. After about six months an idea was formulating in Ted's mind and he began talking to Joyce about it. It was a drastic idea, but he couldn't shake the conviction.

It was on one of their visits with William and Molly that Ted finally broached the subject with them. For the first time Ted revealed that he was considering the ministry. At less than forty he felt he had a lot of productive years ahead, and the desire was like a growing fire within him. William and Molly couldn't have been happier or more supportive.

"How does that fit with the Army?" was Molly's question.

Ted explained that being a chaplain did not seem to be a viable option. Where would a bird colonel with no religious experience fit into the Army's design? It didn't. No, they would have to resign and pursue this course outside of the military. William even called some old friends that he had served with in the military to see if they had any ideas. Some had stayed in the chaplain's corps after WWII. They didn't have any answers for that question. Ted said, "As much as I love the military, Joyce and I are convinced that we can better serve in another way." William assured him he would do all he could to help. He was delighted.

After much prayer, they pursued the goal to get the training needed while he was still in the military. His academic record and achievements at West Point made him acceptable to any college of his choosing and Ted sought to get refreshers in different areas by correspondence before actually applying to a seminary. He couldn't have had a better counselor or advocate than his brother who had his Doctor of Divinity degree. So many doors were opened to him. A plan of action was selected and within six months he was accepted by a Bible college in Kansas City, just fifty miles away. There he could attend evening classes, weekend classes, and from time to time take leaves of absence for more concentrated study. His goal was completion of his theology degree by the time his early retirement came in 1966. Once he had made up his mind, there was no holding back. He was now convinced of what he wanted to do.

With the U.S. becoming more and more involved in Viet Nam, the challenges of the command school offered Ted the opportunity to show his talents. Viet Nam was initially just advisors being sent to bolster and help train the South's military. What started out very small had gained momentum and by early 1963 there were 5000 men in Viet Nam and thousands more on the ships of the U.S. Seventh Fleet patrolling the South China Sea. Time magazine had an article that said, "Such is the war in Viet Nam – a dirty, ruthless, wandering war, which has neither visible front lines nor visible end." This was what the war college at Leavenworth had to prepare commanders for. Ted was in charge of that project.

One of his biggest supporters and encouragers was Gene, the chaplain. His staff saw that the two on-post chapels were properly run and that they ministered to the residents of the prison barracks. With all this, he still took the time to give Ted special consideration and assisted him in his studies, gave guidance, and shared his own years of experience in the ministry with him. This was to end all too soon, however. When the troop level in Viet Nam surpassed 17000 by the end of 1963, Gene received orders to go to Viet Nam. For Ted this was a major disappointment, but the two men vowed to stay in close touch. Ted treasured the friendship and it came as a severe blow when he learned of Gene's death in Viet Nam on his second tour in 1966. He felt that, in a way, his faith was being tested, but he was not deterred. Ted and Joyce did all they could for his family, but there was little they could do to comfort them. People never think about chaplains dying in combat, as though they were immune from danger. In Viet Nam alone, seven died. Six died in combat. Two of them received the Congressional Medal of Honor, the highest honor paid to an American serviceman. Ted was sure that Gene died a hero's death.

Between correspondence courses, night school, and use of accumulated leave time, Ted received his divinity school degree in 1965, six months before he was eligible to retire. Ted's parents were quite surprised at his plans to take early retirement, but they came to accept it. His dad had been a thirty-year man and had always assumed that Ted would be also. In recent years they had seen this son of theirs change, and for the better. They attributed a lot of that to his wonderful wife, but were also finding out more and more about the real change he had undergone. They both let him know that they supported whatever he chose. Their love was unconditional. When Ted's military career came to an end, they packed and headed to Arizona to be close to his folks for a few months before starting his second career. William was lobbying Ted to come to the St. Louis area, but they had decided to delay the decision until they had spent some time with Ted's mother, who was terminally ill. He admitted that the temptation to be near William and Molly was very strong. They enrolled their children in school in Arizona and spent most of their waking hours helping and being with his parents. It turned out to be the last six months of his mother's life and Ted thanked God for sparing her so that he could be with her. She had been ill for over five years but the Arizona climate and her husband's devoted care had prolonged her life much more than the doctors had anticipated. She spent her last months with her son close, his wife, and their grandchildren very near her, as she slowly drifted away. After her death, it was determined that Ted's father would live with them wherever they went from that time on. Jimmy and Casey would have their granddad, and Ted would have the father that wars and military duty had separated him from for so many years.

Chapter 24

☙❧

The Irreplaceable Loss

Life was wonderful for the Swensons. They had never been happier or busier. They had an extraordinary run of good health and had even convinced Leo's parents to rent the home farm out and move to Rockford to be closer to the family. They came in quite handy in caring for the kids and being together only brought the family closer. His parents delighted in the strides that the children were making in school, socially and academically. Both children were gifted and had outstanding talents. William was in seventh heaven because he had grown taller and had become a talented basketball player. He played varsity in his junior and senior years of high school and was elected captain of his senior team. Katie, with her exceptional talent, had a more complex life and one that wasn't easy to program. She required special coaching for her figure skating and that wasn't available in Rockford. Having an ice rink at Rockton, just north of Rockford, was fortunate and sometimes professional talent and coaches were drawn there. This gave Katie an opportunity to learn from them. It was finally determined that they needed to hire a coach and Miss Starka, an immigrant from Romania, was selected. She would travel to Rockford each month and spend three or four days with Katie and lay out the next months plans. Under her tutelage Katie was to become one of the youngest girls to pass the United States Figure Skating Association test, which made her eligible to enter the various national competitions. By the age of thirteen she was landing special ice skating jumps such as the triple salchow, and by fourteen she had mastered the triple toe loop, which girls much older than her had not accomplished. The most unique part of Katie's skating was her emphasis on the spiritual. Her preference was Christian music and she always conducted herself on and off the ice in a manner to honor her gift from God. Some of her peers in the amateur ranks didn't understand what she was doing and a few held her up to ridicule, but she didn't let that stop her. She was a bundle of energy and had the personality of a cheerleader, but she respected her gift and gave her all to the goals she set for herself.

By persevering she won respect from many of her peers and soon was being recognized beyond Rockford as a comer in the profession. Her coach, with the permission of Carol and Leo, set up a plan with the target being the 1968 Winter Olympics. Miss Starka thought she'd be ready despite the fact that she would only be seventeen. In the year and a half leading up to the trials, the schedule would be difficult, but Katie wanted it very much. First, she would have to make a name for herself by competing at various levels of competition, first with the juniors and then with the older group. Judging in figure skating is so subjective that veterans appeared to get the better scores, unless a new skater's reputation for excellence precedes him or her. That was their goal. Create a reputation as one of the best. The plan would involve being away from home and would require tutoring for her classes and financing to cover substantial travel and living expenses. Because Carol and Leo were convinced of her dedication and talent, they knew they would find a way for Katie to compete these next two years until the corporate sponsors and the Olympic Committee itself would take over some of the costs. Help started with her own community. Rockford had heard of her and was behind her and was helpful in the early financing required through various fund raising activities. Things were on track for her goal to be the best she could be.

She had various competitions in the U.S. and Canada over the winter and was entered in the Junior Nationals in Massachusetts in early 1966. The best of the best were present there and at fifteen she was tested to the extreme, but no one outworked her. At the same time she maintained her excellence in her studies. It was the biggest single competition that Katie had ever entered and would mean a lot when it came to getting credentials for the Olympics. Her coach was hearing objections to her choice of choreography and music through the grapevine. Katie stayed true to her convictions and insisted on her spiritual presentation and choice of hymns for her free style skate. She had her mother's support and reluctantly her coach went along. After doing the required figures she skated the free style and finished up second overall in the competition. Some felt that the judging had been unfair, but Katie was happy accepting the silver medal.

It had been an exhausting ninety days on the road. Katie was happy to be going home for a rest and a more normal lifestyle for the next three months. As she prepared for the trip home she noticed her mother did not seem well. She had been so wrapped up in herself that she had missed the fact that her mother was pale and losing weight. She immediately started taking care of her, not allowing her to tote bags or do anything strenuous. She wanted to get her home and get her well. Leo met them at the plane and saw how run down his wife appeared. He put her to bed for two days thinking rest was the best thing. It didn't get better for Carol, so Leo insisted she see a doctor, which she resisted. She had avoided going to doctors all her life and rarely did. Leo kept insisting until she didn't fight him anymore. That's when he knew she was really ill. They ran a barrage of tests and then some retests. The doctors consulted Leo alone and broke the devastating prognosis to him. Carol had an advanced stage case of breast cancer and it had already spread extensively throughout her body. The only thing they could do was to remove as much cancerous tissue as they could to buy her some time. Leo was with the doctor when they told Carol of their findings. He held her as they faced the most trying time of their lives together. The doctor explained that in his opinion they were just buying her some time, maybe three months, maybe six. Initially, Carol did not want the operation, but Leo convinced her to buy all the time she could for the children's sake. They had to be prepared. That evening they sat down with William and Katie and Leo's parents and told them the full story. They didn't hold out any false hopes. The children would have little enough time to adjust the way it was.

She was admitted to the Rockford Memorial Hospital and both breast and extensive lymph node removal were done. The doctors could not say that all the breast cancer tissue had been found and removed, but that had been their intent. Her stay in the hospital for several weeks meant that Leo's parents would move in and help with the children. They did their best to make life as normal as they could for the children, but things were very depressed and difficult. The weeks ran into William's senior year activities, but Carol insisted she be home for his graduation, which she was.

Extensive medication and radiation would have to follow. The weeks and months ahead would be very difficult for Carol. She wanted to be home with her family as much as possible, but at times she was very ill and had to be temporarily hospitalized again. She blamed only herself for neglecting to do the things she should have for early detection, but at no time did she ever say, "Why me, Lord?" She made the children promise that they would look after their own health better than she had.

Carol insisted that Katie continue her training, but Katie would not leave Rockford. Her heart wasn't in it and she refused to go. She would still go to Rockton a few times each week, but that was the extent of her compromise. When the coach explained to Leo and Katie that this would severely curtail her opportunity to make the Olympic Team, that didn't phase Katie's resolve to be with her mother. "I'll practice because I love to skate, but I'll not leave Rockford," was her firm response to her mother. Leo supported her decision.

William had been accepted at Northern Illinois University at nearby DaKalb for the fall semester. He and three of his classmates from high school, Riley, Samuel, and Ross, were hoping to make the basketball team there. His grandfather had helped him secure summer employment with a friend and a farmer south of Rockford where he could room, or drive back and forth, whichever he chose. His dad had gotten him a good used vehicle for graduation. He made the trip home three or four times a week all summer long to be with his mother. The whole family was struggling and they needed to hang together for support. They prayed a lot and the church family helped in many ways.

Carol had been home a couple of weeks when William and Molly drove up from St. Louis for three days to be with her. They were always in touch by phone and waited until what seemed to be the right time to come. Their strength and faith meant so much to Carol and she loved them being there with her. She told her husband, "Their being here means more to me than anyone will ever know. I feel blessed to have this type of family." Carol was finding a new peace in those last days, and when the time came she knew she'd be ready to meet her Lord.

The radiation and medication forced her to stay in bed almost all of the time and she was having rapid weight loss. She took the time she had to prepare her children. She told them how they could help their dad, among other things. She told them how truly proud she was of them and how they should never give up on their dreams. She shared their lives and thoughts and love. At night she would do what she could to raise her husband's spirits. She wanted all of them to get back to a normal life and expressed it. It would be very sad if the kids didn't pursue their dreams and she made Leo promise that he would carry on and be strong for the children. As she grew weaker, the medication had to be increased for the pain and she resisted it as it interfered with her time with her family, but in the end there was no choice. She was in and out of the hospital two times her last month but wanted to be home for the final days. One of the last conversations she had with Leo and the children was to tell them that they were responsible for leading her to Christ, and how lucky she was to have them. It was their lives that had helped change hers.

With her family around her and holding her she died before the leaves had fallen.

Leo's parents were always accustomed to the larger home. On the farm they had more spare rooms than they needed and although it lacked many modern conveniences, this was the lifestyle they were used to. When they moved to Rockford they shunned the apartment or bungalow living in favor of an old two-story home. It was well built, but much too large for an older couple. It seemed foolish at the time to Leo, but it was their choice. Now they persuaded Leo to move himself and the children in with them so that they could help him. Leo's home was too small for all of them to be comfortable, and they had all this space. Leo relented and moved in with them and sold his home.

It was just after Thanksgiving that Katie came to him and asked if it would be possible for her to resume her training with her coach. Leo called Miss Starka and she agreed to pick up where they had left off, even though the lost time would probably make the chances of competing in the '68 Olympics unlikely. She also agreed to perform a guardianship for Katie now that her mother would not be there. In addition, she spelled out what they would need financially to accomplish what they wished to do. Selling the house helped Leo find the finances to at least finance the first six months, which involved foreign travel and training. He would need to do something later to raise more funds, but this at least would get them started. It was still thirteen months before the Olympics began. Two of his brothers had been generous in helping with the extra expense of Carol's illness and final expenses.

Chapter 25

୬୦୦

New Beginnings

It didn't take the Trapp family long to adjust to life in Lawrence. Barb was able to stay home with her baby for the first six months before she started helping out at the restaurant on a part-time basis. There were very few startup or growing pains. Eddie was very happy with the majority of the workers he had hired and they were developing a happy, cohesive group. Eddie's hours were long, often fourteen hours a day, six days a week, but was work that he loved. They closed on Sundays for their sake and also the employees'. He refused to relent to pressure from the public to open Sundays and things had worked out well. On Sundays the family attended Mass together. Eddie had made it clear from the beginning that while he would agree to the children being raised Catholic, he would not consider the possibility of converting himself. He could go to Mass and worship in his own way, and he enjoyed having his family together in worship, but at home he still studied the Bible and talked religion with Barb and the kids and of his beliefs. He wasn't trying to confuse the children, but let them know the alternatives that they might have their own options as they matured. Barb didn't have a problem with his openness.

1963 was a good year and 1964 was even better. By living frugally, in 1966 they were virtually debt free and the restaurant was doing wonderfully. Their restaurant in Cheyenne Wells didn't make it, though. The brother gave up on it and looked for greener pastures. They were fortunate that the pharmacist had been successful and was in a position to buy the entire building from them. With these monies they paid off the mortgage on their Lawrence home. They were comfortable and saw no need to expand their lifestyle. They had been through enough rough years and had learned important lessons. They would never be caught overextended again. They also wanted the kids to have the right values, and material wealth or possessions was never a goal they wanted to stress. The girls shared a room and Eddie built on an extra family room for the growing family. In time, Barb was free to stay at home and raise her family. Eddie could afford a part-time manager and began to free up his weekends and they were able to get away for vacations and visits to see family. They made it back to see Barb's family as often as possible. Life was good and they both knew it was because of the goodness and kindness of the brothers, and they would never forget.

They missed seeing Ted and Joyce after they moved to Tucson. They sure hated to see them go. They got to see William and Molly more than they did Leo because of the distance involved, but they made it a point to drive to Rockford every other year. They corresponded and called more after Carol died and tried to be supportive for Leo and the children. Leo had been down to see them once.

All the cousins delighted in their extended families and made the effort to stay connected. It was as though the special circumstances of their fathers had instilled the need for them to bond even more. Some corresponded regularly and shared each other's joys and problems. They all were in awe of Katie and the celebrity she had become. They hurt with her and William at the loss of their mother. They were disappointed that Katie would apparently have to either curb her ambitions or quit all together.

Eddie had learned of Leo's financial squeeze through William. He was surprised at the magnitude of the financial commitment needed to train a world-class athlete and better understood what Leo was facing. He talked to Barb about what they could do. He was pretty certain that William was interceding and he wanted to help also. They had accumulated a small nest egg in the past two years and now elected to help out Leo. They were sure that the medical bills had taken a toll and this amount, though small, might help. They mailed Leo a cashier's check.

Because Raymond had been his eyes and ears for years in managing the Canaan property, Eddie had the opportunity to call him from time to time. Raymond had been great and a big help. They met for lunch once when they had been visiting Uncle Willis in Charleston, and although Raymond wasn't well, they had a good time talking together. It was from him that he learned of the Trapp family. There wasn't much to know, except of Raymond's father and mother. He had never shared about his family with his boys. The best Raymond could determine, a Hessian soldier brought over to help the English during the Revolutionary War had stayed behind when it was over. He had married an Indian, or whatever passed for marriage at that time, and that was the beginning of the Trapp family in America.

Eddie called Raymond and discussed the possibility of finding a buyer for the acreage and house at Canaan. Raymond thought that could be done without the use of a realtor. The price offered at the time the estate was settled had been very good because of oil speculation on the land, and while there had not been any major hits to date, the possibility still existed. If Eddie wanted to sell, Raymond would contact some people who once showed an interest in it. Eddie asked him to please do so. The situation with Leo's family was such that he and Barb wanted to do something to help. It didn't take long. In less that sixty days they had a buyer at a price almost equal to the original offer made to the estate. The transaction was without complications and there was no gain for tax purposes so all the proceeds could go to Leo. A cashier's check was prepared and sent to Leo for almost $40,000. In his cover note Eddie only mentioned that he was returning a portion of what Leo had given him and Barb. There were no strings attached and they hoped he would receive it in the manner it was given.

Chapter 26

Sharing The Faith

Just prior to taking early retirement and moving to Arizona, Ted heard from his friend Joe Brown. He had not seen the Browns since his last contact with Donna at VMI, and all correspondence had pretty well stopped except for Christmas greetings. In the letter Joe informed him that he was now in command of an army group and it would soon be shipping overseas to Viet Nam. He had attained the rank of brigadier general. He wasn't too enthused with the U.S. involvement there, but his bosses at the Pentagon and the administration thought it was worthwhile to protect the U.S. interest. Joe also felt that Ted was making a huge mistake in taking early retirement instead of sticking it out. He couldn't understand Ted's decision to become a minister and thought he was just bailing out just because of the injustice done to him over the Bay of Pigs.

Joe had said, "I'll soon be in the position to right some wrongs in the Pentagon and we could be a good team again." Ted had written him back thanking him for the thought, but his priorities in life had changed and he was moving on to more satisfying challenges for his and Joyce's life. In his letter Joe had not mentioned Donna and that was not a good omen. Ted was almost afraid to ask. He inquired but didn't receive a response in the six months following.

After his mother passed away, Ted and Joyce had a major decision to make. Personally, the appeal to return to the Midwest to be near William was very tempting, but he wanted to feel his commitment wasn't all about what felt good for them. He wanted his dad with them whatever they did, so the weather was a consideration. The Arizona climate was good for him, so he and Joyce were looking around in the area to see what was needed or where there was a fit for them. In one of his conversations with William the topic of the Philippines came up. A good friend of William's, who was a minister, had started a mission near Manila, and William was excited for him. They had been there six years and had established a mission church, a small hospital, and a Christian school. William's church was helping to support it until it got on its feet. That sounded like a challenge to Ted and he wondered if he should consider that type of ministry. They were talking over dinner one evening and Ted was relaying the facts about the Shelbys' mission in the Philippines when his dad became quite interested in the topic. "They are lovely people," he said. "I spent three tours there, two before the war and one during the war and I wish I could go back some day. Maybe there might even be people that I served with there." Ted and Joyce looked at each other like a flag had been raised. Would this be possible? The next day he couldn't wait to call William and get his thoughts. Would there be a need or room for another mission in the Philippines? William said he would inquire and get back to him. Within a week he called after talking to his friend in Manila. Not only was there a need for more missionaries, but they had a need at their mission. They'd love for Ted to consider serving with them, at least for a while until he decided if he wanted to devote his life to the mission field. Ted could join their efforts and learn the ropes and perhaps one day move on or take over, whatever his calling might be. The idea thrilled them. It would be a big change for the family but Joyce was very enthusiastic about it and the children would adjust. The children were twelve and eight now and this could be such a wonderful learning experience for them. Needless to say, Ted's father was ready to go. In a short time the ball was rolling and they started preparing for the major move. They had physicals to take, shots to get, and furniture to ship. They were taking only the things that had special meaning to them, as the housing might not be as spacious as they were accustomed to.

There was the step of being ordained by the church that needed done. He had his degree and William wanted him to come to St. Louis to be ordained in William's church before leaving for Manila. Ted wanted that very badly.

As it turned out, the trip to St. Louis fit into the plan. Ted's father also wanted to make one last visit to VMI to see old friends before he left. He had spent fifteen years there and Ted understood his motivation for wanting to go. Ted helped set up a reunion with some of his father's old friends and faculty members who were still in the Virginia area. This would allow his father one last visit before departing for what was likely to be his final home. A two-day visit was set up. They'd fly to Virginia, then to St. Louis, be ordained, and go direct to Manila from there. It would be a big adventure for the kids.

The reunion and reception given for Mr. Wainright with two dozen of his friends meant so very much to him. Joyce and Ted tried to stay out the limelight, but he insisted on pulling them in, explaining to everyone their plans and where they were all going in just a couple of days. It was nice seeing old friends, some of which Ted remembered quite well. Donna's parents were there and Ted had a chance to visit with them. They had always been great to Ted and always encouraged him when he was dating their daughter. They didn't have much to say about Donna and Joe except to say that she was visiting them at this time. It was apparent that they were reluctant to talk about them so Ted didn't press the issue. One of the other former faculty members strongly hinted to Ted that he thought Donna "had a problem." Later that evening he and Joyce decided that the right thing to do was for Ted to call her and possibly set up a meeting with her. After all, he had been best man in their wedding and she and Ted had known each other so long. They didn't know why she wasn't at the party. She knew Ted's father quite well. Something was amiss. Ted got her on the phone. Her first words were, "I heard you were back and had hoped you would call. How are both of you?" They talked a few minutes and decided to meet for breakfast at an old haunt near campus that they used to go to.

Donna was still a very attractive woman at thirty-eight, but the eyes had lost their sparkle. She was quick to the point and filled him in on Joe. "Joe's on his second tour of Nam and will be returning in three months. I'll not try to kid you, Ted, things are not going well. We haven't lived as husband and wife for quite a while, but we have no plans to divorce. I understand your life has certainly changed. Who would have thought my first beau would end up a preacher.

Maybe if you'd been a preacher instead of a West Pointer years ago we might have gotten on better. Anything is better than the military." Her attempt to keep things light failed, as underneath it all was an edge of bitterness.

Ted remembered their last meeting. He wasn't much help to her then but knew he had to say something now. "Donna, neither of you have ever met each other half way. What do you do now? Do you work?"

"No, I'm just a social butterfly like I always was, living a useless life and drinking too much. No kids, no direction, and don't care," was her reply. This struck Ted very hard and she noticed his eyes narrowing and bearing down on her, as though he was trying to see inside her head. "Well, I'm surprised you still care, fella," she said.

Ted took a deep breath and started. "Donna, we were too much a like. Immature children, spoiled, selfish and self-centered, thinking the sun came and set to make us happy. I've been lucky. I've had friends and loved ones to help pull me out of self and loved me enough to do so. It took a long time, but eventually I got my priorities straight and now I'm entering into the most exciting time of my life. And do you know what? It isn't too late for you, either. Because I love you, I'm going to give it to you straight. You're deeply loved. Your parents love and worry about you, and your husband loves you very much also. One day he'll get it straight, too. You're both still young and can turn this around. Oh, I don't think he's going to change careers for you and you shouldn't expect it. Have you really found society life fulfilling for you? If so, why are you so empty now? Can't you find a better purpose for your life than what you've been doing? Jesus loves you and wants you to love yourself, because right now you don't. Learn to pray again. Stop the destructive drinking and focus on being the type of person you want to be for your husband and your family. You've been the belle of the ball long enough, and it hasn't fulfilled you. Go over halfway to make someone else happy and you may find it very rewarding. It would be the best thing you'll ever do for yourself, and you can do it. You've always had a tremendous inner strength of character and can change to a better way. I know if you go halfway with Joe, or even more, he'll do the same for you. Do what is best for Mr. and Mrs. Joe Brown. You are worth it." He paused, noticing that Donna was quietly weeping. He covered her hand on the table with his own and sat there until she broke the silence.

"Thanks for coming Ted," she said. "Joyce is a lovely, lucky woman. You deserve each other. I feel where you were talking from and the depth of your caring. That means a lot to me. I'm taking it to heart because I needed someone to say it to me. My parents say it, but we shrug parents off because they have to say it. But you did it out of love and caring and I'll not forget. You could have by-passed me and gone on to the Philippines to do your work, remembering me as the little southern belle of your youth, but you didn't. Thank you for reaching out. This could be the beginning of a change and I want to go home now and write my husband a letter. I haven't written him a letter from the heart for a long time. Maybe he does want to try again. As for you, you're going to be a blessing in a lot of people's lives in your new calling. I'll pray for you and your family as you step out in faith." With that she rose, gave Ted a hug and left the restaurant. Ted looked after her with tears in his eyes and a prayer in his heart for these two friends that had been such an important part of his life.

They returned to St. Louis where the ordination services were a little more than Ted had expected. Unknown to him, William had notified Eddie and Leo and they came with their families for this special day in Ted's life. They had one last dinner together before it was time for Ted and Joyce to move on. All of them being there didn't make the goodbyes any easier, but it was wonderful that they were there. No one could ever know if this opportunity of being together would ever occur again.

It took a full six months to get acclimated to this new life. The Shelbys were wonderful people and helped them to find suitable housing in a safe area where other young families lived. It was unlike anything that either of them had experienced before, but they knew from the start they were going to love it. Ted's dad had been right, these were wonderful people. He had managed to locate a couple of old friends that the general had known during the war. Some of them were top government officials now and expressed their happiness that this old friend had returned to their land. His dad was quick to remind them that MacArthur had said he would return to the Philippines and he did. He hadn't said he would, but came anyhow. The Shelbys could soon tell that they had gotten themselves some excellent help and dedicated servants of God. The Wainrights were ready for the challenge of the rest of their lives.

Chapter 27

కొ∙ఉ

The Power Of Prayer

Some unbelievers would deny the power of prayer. They would scoff at believers who think that prayers are heard. A mother's prayer, no matter how good a mother, would just be wishful thinking. They'd be happy to point out wonderful mothers with dreadful sons and daughters. It would be wrong to say that all prayers are answered in the way we'd like them to be, but prayers of faith are answered. Frances' prayers were answered, not all necessarily as she would have liked, but eventually they were. After her sons, she had grandchildren that went on to be ministers and missionaries. There were nurses, teachers, builders, laborers, researchers, businessmen, and homemakers. They all grew up with a legacy passed on by their parents and one of them even won a medal in the Winter Olympics. We'll never know what their lives would have been like without a mother's prayer, only God knows that. A hero who saved others in the war, a figure skater that glorified God, a foundation that reached out for the needy, The Blessing Restaurant which stands as a tribute of thanksgiving, and a foreign mission that has taken the Word to the lost of the world, educated the young, and helped the sick and homeless. These came from hearts touched by someone, and the believer credits it to God.

Frances wasn't born wealthy. She was brought up in a made-over storage shed. She wasn't beautiful in the eyes of the world. She was looked down on by others and for a crucial time did not like herself. She didn't have an easy life. In fact, it's hard to imagine a mother with a more difficult life. Lost loves and lost children were her lot. She didn't even have an easy death. She suffered. Her dreams were incomplete. What she did have was a praying mother and a faith that sustained her throughout all of her tribulations. She had the assurance that she could say, "If We Never Meet Again This Side of Heaven, We'll Meet on That Beautiful Shore."

Because of a mother's prayer, those that would open their hearts and eyes have an advantage in life. It has nothing to do with health, wealth, or even happiness. It has to do with peace and acceptance and assurance. William was the first of her children to find it as far as we know, but his witness was instrumental in seeing lives changed in Ted's family, Eddie's family, and to a degree, even in Leo's family. William had many privileges in life because of his chance adoption by a wealthy and wonderful God-fearing couple. It wasn't the privileges that he gave credit. He praised God for a mother's prayer.

Chapter 28

༄ ༅

Epilogue

William looked around. In every direction all he saw were groups of women congregating. They weren't playing cards; he didn't see any card tables. They weren't sewing and there wasn't anything tangible in their hands that he could see. They were just standing there in a circle, looking upwards as if in prayer. One group near him looked very familiar. He looked upon their faces and recognized them all. They saw him gazing at them and opened the circle and invited him to come in. He was engulfed by their warmth and love. He was home. He looked upon each face. There were his mothers, his grandmothers, his wife Molly, Carol, and others he had known on earth. They were all so happy to see him. Frances said, "We've been waiting and praying for you, William."

Beyond them he heard a powerful voice say, "Welcome home, good and faithful servant." He felt wonderful and there was such peace.

Someone was shaking his shoulder and he turned his head to see who it was. He had not realized his eyes were closed and so he opened them to see his brothers standing there next to him. It was reunion time again, they had all come.

Leo spoke first. He was totally gray and stooped at the shoulders, but William would have known him anywhere. He was saying, "Go peacefully brother, we'll join you soon. You've been faithful."

Ted spoke next. "Your work on this earth is done, big brother. You can rest in peace now. Your loved ones are waiting. No need to face more pain here."

Eddie took his hand, and William noticed all the while that he'd been lying on white sheets in a bed. "Tell Mom we'll all be there before long, William. She's waited a long time. Her prayer will be answered."

William's lips were moving and they leaned close to hear. "I was just with them fellas. I just saw them all before you woke me up. I've always had wonderful dreams, but I'm not sure this one was a dream. Until then, God bless you." With that he closed his eyes for the last time. One more prayer had been answered.

The End

Printed in the United States
81672LV00002BA/646-660

9 781434 313904